Dream P

'What have you done?' she kept saying over and over again. Then she demanded: 'Do you *know* what you've done?' he felt her beside him, her breath coming in tiny gasps. She gave a little whinny of hysterical laughter. 'Why, you're fiddling while Rome burns!' As she laughed, she hit him hard round the face, time and time again . . .

Also by Anthony Masters

STREETWISE
BADGER

Starling Point Series

ALL THE FUN OF THE FAIR
CAT BURGLARS
SIEGE
AFRICAN QUEEN

Contents

Prologue **Telling the Bees** 7

Part One **Bandstand** 9

Part Two **Stitch-up** 33

Part Three **Echoes** 55

Part Four **Duncan** 71

Part Five **Jack** 97

Part Six **Dead Reckoning** 129

Prologue
TELLING THE BEES

He was playing 'Greensleeves' on the mouth organ to the bees and the walled garden bounced the sound back so that echo followed echo until the clematis-hung masonry seemed to vibrate with the sweet sad notes. He stood over the hives, watching the intricate, industrious world below him.

'What have you done?' Her voice pierced the musical resonance as he knew it would. It had only been a matter of time. 'What have you done?'

He continued playing, listening to her walking quickly down the gravel path towards him. From the hives there came a contented buzz, and the buzzing seemed to fill his head along with the music, blotting out the sound of her crunching, ominously brisk footsteps.

'What have you done?' she kept saying over and over again. Then she demanded: 'Do you *know* what you've done?' He felt her beside him, her breath coming in tiny gasps. She gave a little whinny of hysterical laughter. 'Why, you're fiddling while Rome burns!' As she laughed, she hit him hard round the face, time and time again. He bent away from her blows, too intent on watching the bees to really face the awful reality of her loathing. The mouth organ flew out of his mouth, jarring his teeth, and fell on the gravel. He made a grab for it and stood up. She backed away, thinking that he was going to hit her, but instead he picked up the mouth organ and ran over to the hives.

The echoes of his music still seemed to resound amongst the ancient, weathered walls as he bent over the hive. He turned to face her, but already the soldiers were running through the archway, pointing their guns at him. Meanwhile, a swarm of bees rose and began to collect high above the garden. Soon they formed a tight black cloud in the fading evening heat.

Part One
BANDSTAND

1

There was always the risk that Steve might discover him, yet Woodenbridge dragged Joe back with a will of its own. Inside, he knew that Woodenbridge smelt of cats; outside, of thistles and wild garlic – but for him the deserted house radiated home; the home he had never had; the home he so badly wanted with Kathy.

Now he was tense, listening, waiting for the crack of a twig, the scattering of weed-strewn gravel, the dull thud of a light footstep on the rotting boards of the bridge. The July evening was oppressively hot and nothing stirred, not even a breath of wind. Soon, having heard nothing to alarm him, Joe went into the house and roved around, his slim, almost slight, fourteen-year-old body taut in a combination of anticipation and anxiety. He loved and feared the place, knowing that Steve might come at any time and, if he did, there would be trouble as usual. Sometimes he badly wanted to show Woodenbridge to Kathy, to see if she could share his feelings for it, but most of the time he didn't, for she might either laugh or be afraid. And if he did bring her, he knew Steve would beat him up.

The rooms in Woodenbridge were always cold, and there seemed no central focus, no place for a real gathering. Upstairs the rooms were tiny, but the best part of Woodenbridge was the attic – a huge space that covered most of the house. Curiously, it seemed to have survived better than the rest of the house, but even here Joe knew he was not safe from Steve. There was only one place where he was safe and Joe had named it 'the sanctuary'.

Joe crept down from the attic, went through the kitchen door and was out in the grounds again. Looking round furtively, he hurried towards the overgrown kitchen garden, bent down and cleared away the leaves and foliage which he had used to conceal the entrance. As he sat in the sanctuary, in the small enclosed space with its earthy smell, Joe truly believed that one day he and Kathy would be married and they would make a home together. After all, they loved each other, didn't they? That was half the battle. He closed his eyes and saw the bandstand exploding.

2

Steve Tully stood on the broken wooden bridge that gave the house its name. Below it ran red rusty water. Looking up at the lichen-scarred brick and rotting timber balconies of the house, he swore quietly. Joe would be somewhere in there – he'd been missing since tea. He only seemed to want to be in one of two places: either with Kathy or at Woodenbridge. Steve couldn't think of any way of putting Joe off seeing her and, however many times he beat him up, they were always together. If only *he* could be with her sometimes. He longed to be close to her, to have her for his own . . . Yet when he thought of her again, he felt angry. As if he could beat her too, beat her for preferring Joe.

Steve looked down at the trickle of rusty water flowing low amidst choked banks of nettle and thistle and coarse grass. The wooden slats of the bridge were broken and soft but it was still possible to cross with care. From the bridge he could see most of Woodenbridge. The house was a square brick block with a wooden veranda running round its base. Most of this was covered in ivy now and the tall grasses had taken a stranglehold on the remainder of the shaky structure. But to Steve it was still beautiful and, because Woodenbridge was deserted and no one ever came here except Joe, he saw the place as his own. After all, it nearly had been. The thought always staggered him. Had it not been for what had happened to his grandfather he really could have lived at Woodenbridge. He loved to roam round the wilderness, seeing himself as a lord of the manor, strolling on trim green lawns and up sumptuous servant-lined stairways. He ate in solitary splendour at a long polished table and on the silver plates there was always the most succulent haddock and chips he had ever tasted, followed by shivery orange jelly, tutti-frutti ice cream, hot chocolate and a large brandy.

Steve sat down on the bridge and dangled his legs over the stream. There was a rugby match tomorrow and he would be in the team. Built like a bull, his games teacher had told him. He looked back at Woodenbridge. One day he'd kill Joe. He'd kill him for the way he had not only taken over Kathy but the house as well. He threw a pebble into the water and watched the ripples fan out across the scummy surface. Then he felt in his pocket and pulled out the mouth organ. He began to play and was surprised yet again to find how sweet and sure were the notes that filled his mind.

The visions appeared in the water after the first few bars, just as they had on the TV screen when he played the mouth organ under his desk lid at school. Of course, no one ever *heard* the notes. No one at all, which was just as well, because he had never learnt to play any musical instrument.

In the water he saw his dead parents' wrecked car. Mercifully, it faded after a few seconds. Then Steve saw the face of his brother Duncan. Vaguely, his army uniform shimmered below him. Duncan Tully, the good-looking one of the family. Fine features, sensitive face. Born to command. Steve looked in the water again and saw his own face. For all his good speaking voice, he looked like a punch-drunk boxer. His own face changed to Kathy's, and then again to her body. Her sensuality overcame him and visions and images faded, leaving him hot and desiring her unbearably.

Joe hurried cautiously across the stone-flagged kitchen at Woodenbridge. His trainers made no sound and he felt as if he were walking on air. He looked at his watch. It was almost seven. Mr Sandey, the do-gooder, was going to take them swimming at half-past seven and he didn't want to miss the trip, even if Mr Sandey did smile gravely at him and shake his head and say what a dreamer he was and how was his dad? Joe didn't like to talk about his dad, but Mr Sandey kept on about him because he visited Dad every month. Joe's dad was inside and had been for a long time. He saw him about twice a year when his social worker took him and gradually, with such long gaps between his visits, he had almost forgotten what he looked like. He wanted it that way; what he didn't want was Mr Sandey going on about him.

Joe hurried on over the weed-choked vegetable plot and paused by the tiny walled garden. It was another place he often went into – a suntrap, overgrown with great tall grasses and hollyhocks gone mad. Sometimes he would lie on the ground face-down, pressing his face and hands and legs into the warm scented earth. A strange feeling often overcame him, a feeling of excitement, then climax and then rest.

Tonight Joe just glanced into the walled garden, saw bees buzzing in the evening heat and a couple of daddy-long-legs drifting about as if they were drunk. Blimey, he thought, feeling the sweat between his shoulder blades like clammy hands, they're all drunk on summer. Maybe the air was like wine to the insects, or like the scrumpy cider he and Sean had got drunk on a few weeks ago. 'You'll find yourself in a residential school if you're not careful, Joseph Marney,' Tim who ran the home, had told him before he gated him, and Joe was instantly worried and penitent. If he let them put him away, he wouldn't see Kathy and then life wouldn't be worth living. He'd kill himself by drowning. He'd tried last year, slipping down on to the river bed and watching the waving fronds of weed below him and the distorted translucence of the surface above him. It had been good down there, Joe had thought, as his chest had tightened. Pretty good, and he could put up with the pain. It wouldn't be long before his lungs burst and then he could drift, bumping along the bottom of the river all the way down to the sea he loved. Yes, he thought, as he padded over the grassy gravel, death would be all right. Then he thought of Kathy and sudden joy filled him. Death? Who'd heard of death when love was about?

Joe burst into a run, hoping Steve wouldn't be coming swimming tonight. Last time he'd ducked him *and* punched him in the stomach under water. And when he'd told old Sandey, all he could say to Steve was, 'Watch it, old son.' He would never watch it and if Joe wasn't afraid of death by drowning, he was definitely afraid of death by Steve.

Soon Steve heard the sound of scampering feet. He gave a sigh and was still. Joe was coming down the path and Steve waited, like a praying mantis.

'Gotcha.'

Steve wound a heavy arm round Joe's slim and sallow neck and drew his knee up into the small of the boy's back. Instinctively, Joe grabbed his leg and they both went down into a damp, brambly hollow, narrowly missing the bank of the stream. For a while they lay together, quite still, and all Steve seemed to feel was Joe's light breathing. Then he rolled over and got on top of Joe's now unresisting body.

'I warned you,' he said in his posh voice.

Joe turned his face away but Steve wrenched it back, cupping his chin with his pudgy, strong fingers.

'I warned you.'

Still Joe was silent.

'I said I'd beat you up if I found you here again. Didn't I?'

'Yeah.'

'So – ' Steve ground his knees into Joe's chest and heard the cry of pain with satisfaction. 'You coming up here again?'

'No.'

'Liar.' He ground his knees again.

'I said *no*,' gasped Joe, but they both knew he didn't mean it. Woodenbridge was too important to give up, far too important. Suddenly Steve stood up and dragged Joe to his feet. He shook him like a little terrier.

'You going swimming tonight?'

'Yeah.'

Steve looked at his watch.

'You'll be late.'

Joe wriggled.

'I could keep you here.'

Joe whimpered and Steve suddenly drew him closer.

'What have you been doing here?'

'Nothing,' Joe said sullenly.

'Why do you come here?'

'Gives me something to do, doesn't it?'

'Get going.'

Steve aimed a kick at Joe's retreating jeans but the target was too small and too fast.

'I'll get you,' he said, but Joe was already running over the overgrown path, his legs going like steam hammers. As he ran, Kathy's face swam into his mind and he felt an odd lurching in his stomach. He loved her – he would always love her because she represented all that was secure and loving and lasting in his troubled life.

Steve turned away. The little sod mustn't find out what he was doing here. He went back under the bridge and reached down for the lumpy package. With a shove, Steve pushed it as far back into the hole as he could. As he did so, he swore. If only Joe didn't keep poking around, he could have found a drier hiding place. He had promised Duncan it would be safe and he must honour that promise.

He sat down again, staring into the water, thinking about Duncan. Ever since that terrible night in Germany, when the military policeman had woken them and told them their parents had been killed, they had come to depend so much on each other that other people seemed unimportant. Kathy was the first person that Steve had thought about seriously in all that time.

3

If I ever eat baked beans again, I'll *be* a baked bean. Kathy pushed her long brown hair out of her eyes and scraped the tomato sauce round her plate. The redness suddenly made her think of the exploding soldiers. What did those TV pictures mean? At first it had been surprising, then almost fun. Now it was terrifying. None of the grown-ups knew anything about it. They seemed impervious, but Class 3F, Third Year, Camberley Comprehensive, were not. They were disturbed, waiting . . . but had learnt to hide their fear from teachers and parents.

The soldiers had appeared on their classroom television screen twice this term. The first time, they had been watching a very boring programme on 'A Hundred and One Things to do with Shells'. Suddenly, overlaying the uninfectious enthusiasm of the young cardiganed presenter, appeared the hazy picture of some soldiers falling down the steps of a bandstand. As they fell, there was a kind of indistinct rumbling noise. Then everything went back to normal.

The second time, a few weeks later, they were watching a programme about birth. Just as the cheeky cartoon character, Professor Bonzo, was describing how a baby comes out of the womb, there was a brilliant flash – and the soldiers started falling off their bandstand. When 3F looked more closely they could see legs and arms amongst the smoke but the limbs were not attached to any bodies. Almost immediately they were back to Professor Bonzo. Tim Priestley started to cry but Mrs Hobbins assumed the class didn't like looking at wombs. If only the old bat knew what they had really seen.

The flashes only lasted a few seconds, and the first time Kathy and Joe and everyone else in the class thought they were just passing interference from some other channel. But the second time was too horrible to explain away. The only person who didn't seem interested was Steve. He just grinned and at break-time played the battered old mouth organ he seemed so attached to nowadays. But all the time he looked at Kathy, consuming her with his eyes, steadily working his way into her flesh.

Kathy didn't like Steve because of the way he treated Joe, but there was more to her dislike than that, although she couldn't exactly explain it. All she knew was that she often hated Steve and his lumpen body with a deep dark hatred that worried her. At other times he attracted her. Not that she was going to admit that – not even to herself. As for Joe – he haunted her. To Kathy, he was so special that she could hardly bear to think of him in case he went away.

Kathy couldn't bear to think of the soldiers either, because it frightened her too much. Her mother had great perception and could usually winkle things out of her, mostly from the expression on her face, but she didn't want her to know about them. Especially now, because of Joe, Kathy realised more and more that she had to barricade herself against Mum.

Kathy had never had a dad. There was just her and

Mum, and, of course, Gran. Fourteen years ago Gran had been scandalised by her daughter 'carrying on' and giving birth and keeping the baby 'without a thought to the consequences', but now she treated Kathy in a rather sickly adoring way and would often try to take her on her knee where she would cluck at her like a sad old hen. Gran blamed 'him' for all Kathy's defects: her plain face with its snub nose, her too-large lips and deep-set eyes. They had all been endowed by 'him'.

Gran, thought Kathy, was yuk, and she hated her for the rotten patronising way she treated Mum. But what really worried Kathy was her mum's lack of social life. She worked in a small estate agent's office and at the weekends she gardened and cooked and cleaned and made a home for Kathy. Kathy knew she was lonely and cornered; so much so that she forced herself through each day, living for the moment, finding sanctuary in a routine that she was terrified to break out of. But Mum wasn't repressive and home was open house to all Kathy's friends. Then Joe had turned up, and open house didn't apply to him. Mum just didn't want to know. A boy from the community home? No takers.

Gran abruptly left the table, saying that she was having 'one of her turns'. Once she had gone, Mum and Kathy caught each other's eye and burst into subdued giggling. It was wonderful, that kind of laughter. Intimate and delicious. Gran's 'turns' were all too regular and entirely the result of overeating. Why can't we have more of this laughter? wondered Kathy. Much, much more. Of course they had when Mum was younger and before Gran came to live with them. Then there had just been the two of them, laughing and sharing all the pains and joys. Games in the park, jaunts to the seaside, Saturday evening cinema-going, fish and chip suppers – it had all been so good. Then Gran had arrived like an old grey ghost and had begun to suck all the lifeblood out of Mum.

4

Days passed before anything else happened. Then, on one particularly overcast morning, Kathy had a sense of foreboding as she trailed into the school buildings. They were very drab and always gave her the impression that she was nothing, as she joined the herd that swarmed the wide corridors, asphalt playgrounds and revolting loos.

Kathy hated the school with its continual atmosphere of despair. Despair for the kids, that they wouldn't pass exams or get jobs, and despair for the teachers, who knew they couldn't teach them and didn't have the morale or intelligence to do so anyway. It was a tight little world which she longed to break out of, and she would, too, before it got to her. She would run away with Joe. It was all a dream, of course, but a good one.

On that morning Kathy's instinct and her slight apprehension suddenly grew stronger and she realised that she was now almost willing something to happen. Anything would relieve the trough-like boredom of walking through the school corridors, day after day, and smelling the same smells and seeing the same people and learning the same safe dull things. As for the teachers – well, it might be quite nice if *they* all lost arms and legs. Not that she really meant it, of course, and she didn't want to be so wicked, but there was Mrs Jackson (English) with her bright, matter-of-fact 'I'll give you a bit of common sense' and the hard, bright, chirpy voice that droned on and on. Kathy hated her mainly because she was so boring. Once a supply teacher had come to the school and she had talked to them about her mum dying of cancer, which had been great because it was brave and true. But Mrs Jackson gave them hard, shiny, common sense and that was awful.

'Joe.'

He turned towards her in the corridor, his eyes smiling, and a thrill went through her, as if by his very presence they could look at the world and laugh at it together. Together, they went into registration and listened to Mr Edwards urging them to go on a fun run. Then they went into the first class.

'Fun run,' muttered Joe. 'Not likely.'

They should be on a beach together somewhere, she thought, having a fun run. And then they would lie in the dunes.

'Will it happen today?' she breathed.

He grinned at her in return. Did he have green eyes?

'It might happen,' he whispered back as Mrs Jackson shrilled: 'Morning all. Now sit down, and I don't want any talking.'

They ignored her, all of them, knowing, as she did, that she would have to yell at them another couple of times to get silence. Her voice was like an air-raid siren, thought Joe, the ones he had heard on telly, or like a burglar alarm that you ignored in the street.

'Will you shut up!' she shrilled and eventually they did. 'Today we're going to look at a new schools programme about Dylan Thomas and there are new books to go with it. Now, open them up at the first page and remember these have got to be covered by you tonight at home.'

She droned on about Dylan Thomas. Who is he? wondered Kathy. Some Welsh git, thought Joe. Simultaneously they both looked across at Steve and saw that he had his desk lid open. Underneath it, he put the mouth organ to his lips. Surely he's not going to play it now, thought Kathy, and Joe nudged her, obviously thinking the same thing.

A few minutes later, after some bright and boring patter from Mrs Jackson, the television screen flickered into life with a picture of Larne harbour, and a man strode across the screen and stood on the mud. He began to talk about Dylan Thomas in a bright, lively and patronising way, rather like Mrs Jackson. Kathy had the impression that he was looking for some nice little box to put the poet in. Pity, she thought as Dylan Thomas' picture flashed up, he looks rather nice.

She yawned and again looked across at Steve and saw that he was actually blowing into his mouth organ. No sound emerged, but he still looked as if he was playing a tune and his eyes were bright with the music. Then Mrs Jackson saw his desk lid was open and shouted at him to close it. Grinning, he did as he was told, but his foot kept tapping. Kathy felt a sudden lurch in her stomach. Somehow she knew it was all going to happen. There was a quiet smile of understanding playing on Steve's face as the television screen grew hazy and Larne harbour was replaced by the shadowy image of a marching band of soldiers. There was no sound and they seemed to be marching up a sweeping gravel drive. Then, to Kathy's amazement, she could see the insubstantial forms of Mum and Gran amongst a crowd at the top of the drive. She was sure it was them, and soon there was no doubt at all as the picture clarified and closed in on Gran. Her mouth was opening and closing rapidly and she had that shrewish look in her eye that Kathy had grown so used to, while Mum had her habitual patient, long-suffering expression as she bore the brunt of a full flood of typical Gran harangue. There was no sound, but Kathy could hear it all inside her head.

'There's my mum,' hissed Joe suddenly, and Kathy turned to look at him in bewilderment. He was shaking and there were tears in his eyes and she began to realise that all the class could see their parents in the crowd – dead or alive. Some children were already crying, but they couldn't wrench their eyes away from the screen and no one gave a thought to Mrs Jackson.

When she turned back to the television screen the scene had changed. The soldiers were sitting on the bandstand near the veranda of an ugly, rambling, old house. The sun was shining, the band was playing and she could see Mum and Gran looking on. Then came the flash of the explosion and the whole class cried out in one howling, protesting voice. As they did so, Larne harbour came up through the smoke.

'You know, it was really funny,' chattered Mrs Jackson to a colleague in the staff room at coffee break, as they both drank mauve-grey coffee and ate soft, stale, digestive biscuits, 'Graham Markham was reading from Thomas on the box. I've never liked his delivery, but it certainly seemed to turn on my kids.'

'What was he reading?'

'Fern Hill.'

Mrs Jackson was eager to quote:

> *'Now as I was young and easy under the apple boughs*
> *About the lilting house and happy as the grass was green,*
> *The night above the dingle starry,*
> *Time let me hail and climb – '*

Her voice trailed away.

'Did they understand it?'

'Understand it? All their little eyes were filled with tears and some of them simply sat back and howled.'

'How extraordinary.'

'Wasn't it?' She paused and thought, and then added excitedly: 'I say, do you think poetry is getting to them at last?'

5

Joe and Kathy cycled slowly over the heath. They didn't have much time as Mr Sandey would be fetching Joe for swimming at seven. But they had to be by themselves. The events at school that day had been so extraordinary that they still felt numb. 3F had met in the playground, hardly speaking to each other, but staying together for mutual safety. Gradually, a few members of the group moved away and idly kicked a ball, whilst others played an apathetic game of tag. The majority just stood and thought and tried not to believe in what they had seen: the dearest people in their world killed in some nightmare. Then the bell went and they stumbled through the rest of the school day and hurried home to make sure that they had really been dreaming. They knew they had, but what they could not make out was why they had dreamed, and why they had seen a vision, and why they had all shared it, yet were so unable to speak to each other about it. Not so Joe and Kathy.

'What the hell is it all about?' said Kathy.

Joe shrugged and the slight lilt in his voice made her feel as if she wanted to throw her arms around him. 'We all saw a vision. It must mean something. Do you think it's going to happen, in the future?'

'But why should Mum and Gran get blown up while they're watching a band?'

'My mother walked out on us,' said Joe quietly. 'I don't know where she is.'

Kathy felt the tears at the back of her eyes. She knew his mother had gone but he had never told her.

They paused by a dried-up pond. This was a blazing summer of appalling heat and the landscape seemed burnt out around them. As they sat on the hot grass by the dry bowl of the pond, Kathy felt an onrush of fear. She turned to Joe for comfort, knowing that in his small frame there was a great strength that was for her and her alone. When they had first met she had been drawn to him immediately. She had never had a boyfriend before and had never contemplated having one. She didn't have all that many girlfriends either, for she had never been very outgoing. But Joe was special and so different because of – well, what was it? – it was very hard to put into words. She occasionally wondered if he had cast a kind of spell over her. Sometimes he was quiet and companionable and she didn't feel she had to talk to him, rather that they could be near to each other's thoughts. At other times he could be volatile, flying off the handle over little things, or passionately defending some point of view that he didn't really believe in or think was that important anyway.

He was such a strange mixture of inwardness and outwardness and she never really knew how he was going to react. But he lit up her life. She remembered the phrase from a tape she had heard of a West Indian Spiritualist Meeting: 'You light up my life'. The fact that Joe lived in a children's home and that his dad was in prison and his mother had gone away must be so awful. It must be even worse to live in the same place as Steve. For some months now she had nurtured the mad idea that she could persuade Mum, and even Gran, that Joe should come and live with them. But that was impossible. Gran deeply disapproved of their friendship. 'He's a bad lot,' she moaned. 'A boy in a home with a father in prison. No good will come of this,' she had pronounced. 'Mark my words!'

She and Joe often wrapped their arms around each other and kissed; the quick, dry kisses Kathy found so beguiling that she longed to make love to him and feel his slim wiry body close to hers. As she looked at the dry grass and smelt the burnt gorse, desire rose up in her until it was almost unbearable. But, as always, they would touch and lean and kiss and nothing more. It was not like saving anything up; it was just a barrier that they wanted to break but couldn't, for some reason that neither of them could understand. Perhaps because, once crossed, there would be no paradise left to enter. Often when she desired him so much, Kathy would ask Joe to talk about the village in Northern Ireland where he had lived until he was ten, when his mother had gone away. Soon after that he and his dad had come to England and, almost immediately, his dad had blundered into some serious trouble. Joe would never talk about that, but Kathy knew by instinct that it had been violent and horrible.

'Tell me about Kerryside,' she said.

'Not again,' he laughed, but she knew that he, like her, loved to talk about the village, Kerry, the dream palace of his childhood. He began to talk in his light and lovely voice.

'The harbour wall ran right out into the spray and we used to stand up there, getting the salt in our mouths and fishing. As often as not, there was a rain mist, too, and it blotted out the hills behind us in a funny kind of purply grey . . .'

As his soft voice cooled the hot landscape, Kathy made love to him on a purple-grey hillside overlooking the sea, whose song entered them as they stroked each other in the rain. Gone was the arid and acrid heat of Camberley and in its place was the soft mist of make-believe.

For make-believe it truly was. Joe had never been brought up in an Irish fishing village, but rather in the Divis flats in Belfast. His mother really had walked out on them. Joe's dad had never been part of the Troubles, despite the fact that they were Catholics and surrounded by agitation and intimidation. When the Troubles threatened to close in on them, they came over the water. Once in England, Joe's father got himself a job as a waiter at a posh steak house in Guildford. He could have risen to the rank of head waiter if he had not been involved in a burglary and had beaten a man half to death.

Kathy was Joe's saviour and the invented past of Kerry was something they both needed. He, because it gave him romance and identity and actual happiness and she, well, he couldn't even guess at the reasons but he knew that they were very strong, whatever they were. Now, as they sat on the grass and smelt the scorched earth, Joe went on talking about Kerry and they both forgot everything else.

'And I'd go down with my da and bring in the catch sometimes, and we even used to go out on the trawlers and haul up the nets. Then we'd sell the fish on the quayside, and after that we'd walk back to our cottage that was just behind the pub on the strand. And in the evening Da and I would go walking on the sand when the tide was out and we might dig for lug and then . . .' His voice lilted on and Kathy closed her eyes, seeing only Kerry and not his lies. She was almost asleep when she felt Joe nudging her.

'Yeah?'

'Something I didn't tell you.'

'Eh?'

'About what we saw on the telly. That bandstand and the explosion an' all.'

'So?' She was sitting up now, trying to take notice.

He was silent for a moment and she pushed at him impatiently.

'Well? What are you on about?' She was still full of Kerry and didn't want to be dragged back to the menacingly inexplicable.

'The bandstand. It really existed.'

Suddenly she was with him and her chest tightened up until she felt there was a bandstand inside her.

'Existed? What do you mean?'

'There's an old house called Woodenbridge – '

'I know it.'

'I often go there when I'm lonely.'

'I *didn't* know that. Why didn't you tell me?'

'That I was going up there?'

'That you were lonely,' she said fiercely.

He shrugged. 'Anyway, the bandstand – '

'Well?'

'There was one at Woodenbridge. The soldiers used to play on it and all the local people would come and listen.'

'Are you sure it's the one we saw?' Her voice was toneless.

He shrugged again. 'I don't know. All that's left of it is covered up by long grass.'

'What do you mean "all that's left of it"?'

'It was in a book Tim, my housefather, lent me about Camberley. Someone blew it up while the soldiers were playing on it.'

'Why?' She was shivering now, despite the heat.

'They had a grudge,' Joe said at last. 'I've got to go, Kathy. Mr Sandey's taking me swimming.'

Why couldn't he tell her what he'd read? He'd learned it by heart, for some reason he did not understand.

'If you must. At least we'll see each other tomorrow, whatever happens.'

Once in his room Joe opened *The History of Camberley* on the page that fell open so easily.

> *'Woodenbridge House. Originally built in 1873 in a mixture of styles by Captain Andrew Tully, the house is best remembered for a tragic incident in 1922 when the Camberley Military Band were the victims of a home-made bomb while playing the tune "Greensleeves" at Woodenbridge on a summer Sunday evening. Captain Tully had erected a large, lavishly proportioned bandstand on the lawn. It had been his custom to throw open the house and grounds to selected guests from the local neighbourhood and it had been on one of these occasions that the tragedy took place. In all, sixteen soldiers and twelve members of the public were killed, whilst many others were badly injured.*
>
> *'Some days later, Lieutenant Jack Tully, eldest son of Captain and Mrs Andrew Tully, was arrested and accused of being the perpetrator of the incident. He was convicted at Guildford Assizes and hanged on October*

14th, 1922. Tully's motives were never entirely clear, although it was stated in his defence in court that he had been chastised in some way by brother officers at Camberley barracks.

'Popular rumour has it that when soldiers arrived at Woodenbridge to arrest him, Jack Tully was playing a mouth organ to his wife in the walled garden.'

Joe turned over on his back because there was something bothering him. A link? What could it be? Steve's face swam into his mind. Steve Tully!

Joe shut the book and lay on the bed face-down, thinking about Kathy. He felt tired, washed out. He looked at his watch and heard a movement at the door. There were only six children in Rivermere, including him and Steve, and each had a separate bedroom. Privacy was of the highest importance to Joe, so he was annoyed to look up and see Mr Sandey standing there.

He was quite old and always smiling, with a long pink face, not much hair and a little moustache that looked like a very thin, very tired mouse. Once Mr Sandey had put his hand on Joe's leg in the swimming pool in a funny way and Joe had told him to go away. Although Mr Sandey had never touched him again, Joe knew he was biding his time. But he and the other young ones from the home kept going swimming with him because the care staff were a bunch of idle layabouts and never took them, not if Mr Sandey was sucker enough to do so. Joe, who loved swimming, wasn't going to miss out, Mr Creepy Sandey or no Mr Creepy Sandey.

He was looking particularly creepy this early evening with his mac, gnome-like features and confiding manner.

'Sorry. I knocked but you couldn't have heard.' His voice had a slight whine to it and Joe shuddered.

'OK.'

'Saw your dad last week.'

'Yeah.'

'Sends his best.'

'Yeah.'

'Want to talk, or be alone?'

'I'm easy.'

Mr Sandey sat on the bed and Joe could smell his stuffy raincoat.

'He may get parole in a couple of years.'

A couple of years seemed a lifetime to Joe and he said nothing.

'Want to go down the baths tonight?'

'Don't mind.'

'The others have had enough for this week, so it's just you and me.'

'Yeah?' Joe was hesitant.

'I've asked Tim and he said you could go if you want.'

'Well . . .'

Mr Sandey caught hold of Joe's ankle and held on to it. His grip felt soft and slimy.

'I'll come,' said Joe and Mr Sandey let go.

'I've got another treat in store for you.'

'What's that, then?'

'How about coming up to the barracks some time?'

'OK,' shrugged Joe. 'Don't mind if I do.' Anything to shut him up, thought Joe. Anything to get him off my back. He wanted to think about Kathy, and old Sandey was getting in the way. Let him buzz off, the old pervert. There was a yearning inside him and he didn't know how to control it. It was a terrible longing for Kathy, and it wouldn't go away. He wanted to take her in his arms and be close to her. But he wouldn't do the other things. He couldn't. It would spoil it. Like telling her Kerryside didn't exist.

Part Two
STITCH UP

I

There were not many people in the swimming pool changing rooms. Joe's eyes were sore with the chlorine and as he tugged on his clothes he was very conscious of old Sandey standing nearby with a towel. Joe had his own towel so there was no need for Sandey to stand around, but Joe knew that he had to have the excuse of a towel to be there at all. Then he could hear Sandey's ancient old tennis shoes – he never seemed to wear anything else – dragging their way towards him. The half-door whipped open and Sandey groped his way inside, flicking the towel at him in a mock challenge to battle. He looked very disappointed when he saw that Joe was dressed and Joe almost laughed aloud. The old fool couldn't even get his timing right.

Steve was aware that the time had come to do what Duncan had told him. It was a pretty crazy joke and at first he had just laughed at him. But now he could see it was a good idea to give the nasty child molester, Sandey, the scare of his life.

Steve was aware that every time old Sandey returned

to Rivermere he would go to talk to Tim about whatever protégé he happened to have at the time. Somehow he needed to justify himself, thought Steve, as he watched him march through to Tim's office with a cheery smile and a wave to Joe who darted upstairs to his bedroom. Everyone knew about old Sandey, with the exception of Tim and his staff who never seemed to have the slightest suspicion. He had a wife he often brought into the home and Steve reckoned it was this respectable front that saved him. Good cover job, they all thought. If you were married, you couldn't be queer.

Steve had seen Sandey leave his car at the back of the house and it didn't take him more than a minute to run down the side passage and get underneath the chassis. He spent two or three frantic minutes before he was able to drag himself out, unseen. Waiting until he had finished panting, Steve strolled back into the house, but there his luck ran out and he spent ages hanging around outside Joe's room, waiting for him to go downstairs for cocoa. But at last Joe came out and thundered downstairs, leaving Steve with the coast clear.

Tim Johnson breathed a sigh of relief as Mr Sandey reluctantly left his office and went outside into the sweltering night to get into his car. Tim swore and poured himself a large whisky and then sat at his desk, relief sweeping over him. Sandey was a nice enough old boy, pillar of the church and much respected up at the barracks where he was a security guard at the gate. His wife was a good sort too, quick to fund-raise and support Rivermere in any way she could. Collectively and individually, the Sandeys took the kids on outings and had even been known to undertake temporary foster jobs. They were goodhearted Christian people and there weren't many of them left, thought Tim. All the same, the old man didn't half go on. Suppose he was lonely in a kind of way, despite his old woman. Their children were grown up, perhaps that was why they both doted on the Rivermere kids. Tim poured himself another whisky and opened up a copy of *Child Care*. He'd been at Rivermere too long; it was time to think about moving on.

Steve couldn't sleep and he continually turned and sweated as he realised what he had done. However much he wanted to please Duncan, however much he hated Joe and desired Kathy, the sheer scale of his action was unbelievable. Eventually he rose and crossed to the window. He looked out into the hot night where not a blade of grass stirred. He longed for the winter and the gusty rain that often shook the ill-fitting windows of Rivermere. He could not bear the total lack of movement, the thought of what was going to happen. But Duncan had wanted it to happen – and whatever Duncan wanted, Steve had to carry out.

After a while Steve went back to bed and dreamed of Kathy. It was a good relaxing dream and it obliterated all reality. He and Kathy were the lord and lady of Woodenbridge. The house was no longer a ruin; it had been transformed into a kind of turreted fairy-tale castle, with lawns sweeping down to a crystal lake. On the lawn was a bandstand and, on summer nights, an orchestra would be arranged in front of it, with servants lining groaning tables of food behind. Now he and Kathy were dancing alone on the bandstand to the tune of 'The Blue Danube'. When they had finished everyone clapped and they went to the tables for fish fingers and ice cream and brandy. Yes, it was a good dream.

* * *

Mr Sandey took the bend slowly but opened up on the last straight before plunging downhill to the small, tidy estate on which he and his wife had lived for the past twenty years. He was thinking about Joe when he put his foot on the brake for the first time during the journey. It did not connect and he tried again, still thinking about Joe. Then the whole pedal went flat to the floor and the old Escort sped towards the corner. He jerked the pedal again and again, up and down, up and down. Just as he realised his efforts were useless, he went into the final corner. Somehow, he steered round most of it, and was almost within sight of home when he saw the truck coming slowly towards him. A few seconds later they collided head-on and Mr Sandey disappeared through the windscreen.

2

The school day had not been so bad, Joe thought as he cycled home. Nothing had happened to the classroom television set and he had seen Kathy alone at break-time. They had wandered round the edge of the games field in contented silence.

When Joe saw the police car standing outside Rivermere he was not particularly concerned. The kids were always up to something and quite often one of them was done for thieving. He had not got involved in anything like that since he had started going out with Kathy. There just didn't seem to be any need, somehow.

Putting his bike up against the wall, Joe sauntered into the hallway. It was empty and for a moment Joe had the funny feeling that it wasn't real. But there was the same old grandfather clock without one of its hands, the brown paint, the picture of the Monarch of the Glen, the dusty sideboard with lots of pictures of kids taken over the years, the notice board with admonishing notices from Tim, and the roller skates. Yet now it seemed like a stage set. Then, quite suddenly, it was as if the actors had arrived. Tim and two coppers stepped out of his office. They stared at Joe in a rather puzzled, sad way.

'Hi, Joe. Can you come in for a sec?' Tim's voice sounded forced.

As Joe followed them inside the office, he saw Steve coming down the stairs. There was a grin on his face and for a moment he stared straight into Joe's eyes. Joe felt the first beginnings of fear begin to creep over him.

Inside the tiny office Joe immediately sensed the tension and the kind of foreboding that had filled him when he'd had to talk to the police before. Then he'd known he couldn't win; they either had proof against him or they were going to get it out of him anyway. But this time he was sure he hadn't done anything at all.

Tim looked very pale and, as he rested his hand on the desk, Joe could see that his little finger was shaking badly. He made a conscious attempt to force his voice to sound as normal as possible and failed dismally.

'Joe.'

He paused and Joe stared back at him.

'Yeah?'

Joe turned to gaze at the policemen. One was rather old, kind and fatherly-looking. He seemed sad and worried. The other policeman, however, was much younger. He looked brisk and questioning and somehow contemptuous. Joe was instantly terrified of him.

'Mr Sandey's been involved in an accident. An

accident in his car.' Tim paused and swallowed. 'He's on the danger list.'

'Yeah?' Joe could think of nothing else to say. He felt totally bewildered, but the sense of foreboding was increasing rapidly.

'The police checked over his car and found that the brake cable had been cut.' Tim swallowed again. 'Something's been found in your room.'

'Something?'

'A dirty penknife with brake fluid on it.'

A kind of blackish-reddish haze descended over Joe's mind and hot angry tears sprang to his eyes.

'I never touched his car.'

'Steve says he saw you climbing out from underneath it last night, and so does Dave.'

Dave would say anything Steve told him to, thought Joe miserably. Anything.

'I'm being stitched up.'

'We want to ask you a few questions, son,' said the older policeman, sitting on the edge of Tim's desk. 'Just a few questions.' But Joe could feel the younger policeman's eyes boring into him and he knew that he was being softened up.

Kathy met Mum after school; they went shopping and then to the Brown Owl Café for a cup of tea. This was becoming a regular habit – a regular truanting from Gran's miserable regime at home. She had taken them over completely and she treated Mum as a child and Kathy as a burden. So while they were together, around the shops or the café, places where Gran's arthritic legs wouldn't get at them, they felt a new kind of freedom – a freedom that had become addictive. They would linger in Marks and Sparks, window-shop in Debenhams, and order yet another pot of tea in the Brown Owl. And it was here that Mum would talk about the past, escaping back into it, and Kathy would wallow in the secondhand nostalgia.

Today she was telling her about her dad and how, at a time when Mum had been lonely, they had met at a disco and made love in a car park.

'I never saw him again,' she said.

In fact, Mum had told Kathy the story of that love-making many times before but it didn't matter. It was part of their shared happiness. They had their own secrets – and a special private world into which Gran could never intrude.

Regretfully they finished the last of their brackish tea and prepared themselves for arid reality again.

3

'Nasty crash on Tanner Hill last night.' Mum was boiling haddock for tea and Gran sat at the table like an old hooded crow. She must have been a handsome woman once, thought Kathy, but now her face was deeply lined. She had been tall, but now walked and sat with a permanent stoop that made her look like a bird of prey. Mum was like a little hedge robin, dominated by this larger, crueller bird.

'They say the driver might die,' croaked Gran, looking round the tea table as if searching for carrion. 'You'd never get out of that lot alive.'

Mum clucked in return, as if relishing titbits, although Kathy was sure that they were the kind of titbits that weren't pleasant to eat. Kathy remembered how Gran had always forced them to eat up bits of gristle and fat. 'They're the titbits,' she had said. 'They're the bits that are good for you.'

'It's a nasty corner,' said Mum. 'A very nasty corner.'

'It'll take more lives,' pronounced Gran with relish. She buttered a piece of new loaf and bit into it with grim satisfaction. It was amazing; Gran had kept every tooth in her head and they were as sharp as they had been when she was a girl. She was immensely proud of this fact and Kathy sometimes wondered if she sharpened them up at night with a chisel in her glory hole of a bedroom. An eagle's nest, thought Kathy, full of carried off prizes.

The telephone rang and Mum moved to the hall to answer it. She returned quickly.

'It's Joe,' she said.

Gran cleared her throat like a rasp.

'Yes?'

'Joe.'

'Hi.'

'There's trouble.' His voice was faint and tentative.

'What kind of trouble?'

'Big.'

'What's up?'

'Old Sandey . . .'

'Who?'

'He's an old boy who takes us swimming. He took me last night.'

'And?'

'His car crashed.'

'Tanner's?'

'Yeah.'

'Last night? Gran's full of it.'

'He's hurt real bad.'

'Were you with him?'

'No.'

'Then?'

'They think I messed up his car. Did something to the brakes. And they found a penknife in my room.'

'Penknife?'

'It was filthy and covered in brake fluid.'

'Blimey!'

'I've been stitched up.'

'Who by?'

'Steve. I'm sure it's him.'

Kathy felt a surge of fear. Steve was becoming too powerful in their lives.

'Why?'

'He grassed on me, and got another kid to grass on me too.'

'Are you sure?'

'I didn't do it.' His voice broke. 'Don't you believe me?'

''Course I do,' Kathy said firmly.

There was a long silence.

'Want to come round?' she asked. He ignored her.

'They want me to go down the nick.'

'Oh.'

'If I go down there, I'll never get out.'

'Why?'

'I'm being stitched up, aren't I?'

Kathy didn't know whether he was or not, but she did know that he sounded like a trapped animal. Suddenly her heart went out to him and she wanted to take him in her arms. For a few fleeting seconds she thought of telling Mum and then remembered Gran and decided against it.

'What are you going to do?'
'Run for it.'
'What?'
'Run.' His voice was bleak and desperate.
'Where?'
'Back home. To Kerry.'
'Kerry?' Her heart missed a beat. 'You'll never do it.'
'No?' His voice took on an unlikely assurance. 'I've been on the run before. Know my way around.'
'Before?'
He didn't answer. Then said, 'I want you with me.'
She didn't immediately understand what he was saying.
'I want you to run away with me,' he reaffirmed.
She didn't reply for a few seconds and Joe stayed silent too. In the other room she could hear Gran say: 'Whatever *is* that girl doing? If she thinks she's going to have a life of her own at her age she's got another think coming.'
It was this announcement that finally made Kathy determined to join him.
'Where are we going?' she hissed.
'To Kerry.'
'You mean – you and me, in Kerry. We'd be caught.'
'No way. Trust me for the journey, and when we get there. It's a tiny place.'
'We'd be noticed more in a tiny place.'
'Not in my log cabin.'
'Cabin?'
'My da's got a cabin on the shore.'
This was all mad, thought Kathy. All mad. Yet a terrible excitement filled her. They would be together on an adventure.
'What happens if I don't come?'

'I shall still go,' he said brusquely.

So there it was. She thought of a life without Joe. School and Gran. It would be impossible.

'I'll come.'

Once she had said the words, a number of different emotions passed through Kathy's mind, the chief of which was a riveting fear. Then, just as quickly, it vanished and she could only think of the sand dunes of Kerry and lying in them together. Living in the cabin would be like playing real life, and that's what she wanted – she and Joe together, whatever the dangers. But then the fear returned and she knew whom she was really afraid of: Steve.

'We'll have to hide out for a couple of days first,' said Joe.

'Where?'

'I know somewhere.'

'When?'

'Now. After a few days they'll stop watching the ports so closely.'

'Yes,' she heard herself saying. 'Yes, I'll come.'

'Meet me in half an hour by the rec. Don't be late.'

As she rang off, Kathy's thoughts changed again as she plummeted into reality. It was all crazy. Of course she couldn't go with him. But as everything had been so crazy recently, anything was possible. She remembered the bandstand. Could it have been real, once?

Of course she wouldn't go with him, Kathy thought as she tried to eat her tea. She chewed leathery fish under the eagle's eye and felt more and more constrained. Then Gran and Mum started some silly argument.

'You know these came from Bond's. You should have

got them from Harrison's,' grumbled Gran as she picked at her fish.

'They came from Harrison's.'

'They're Bond's.'

'They came from Harrison's, Mother, I swear it.'

'I'd know haddock from Bond's anywhere.'

'Mother, I tell you . . .'

Their voices bickered on but Kathy was not hearing them. Instead, she saw a wild Irish Sea and a strip of fresh sand and a dancing wind. On a clifftop she saw a log cabin and inside a fire burned in the hearth. In that moment she knew it was a dream, Joe's dream, not hers, but to follow it was to escape the unrelenting boredom of her life, and the remorselessness of Gran, and the inadequacy of Mum.

Kathy suddenly saw a vision of herself sitting at this table eating haddock in twenty years' time. Gran would be the same because she was magically ageless, Mum would be older and she herself would be sitting in a lumpy sweater and a sat-out skirt around the table of skirmish: three generations of women sitting at the table with hopelessness in their eyes. It was like being trapped in hell. And the dream? Well, it would no doubt lead to trouble, but there was a reality and it was Joe.

'Come on, my girl,' said Gran. 'Stop dreaming and make some conversation.'

But the only thing that Kathy could think of saying was: 'Are you never going to die?' And as she couldn't very well say that, she said: 'I'm going out after supper, Mum.'

'Where to?' asked Gran aggressively.

'Just to play badminton with Angie.'

'Finished your homework?' asked Mum.

'Yes.'

'Then I don't see why not.'

Gran scowled. Then she said: 'Go on, you need the exercise. You're getting fat – and your hair – '

Kathy hurried from the table, pleased with her decision. Whatever Joe had done, and she knew he was innocent, whatever they were about to do together, nothing could be worse than this.

Steve lay on his bed, trying to keep out the thought of what he had done to Mr Sandey. Instead, he saw himself with Duncan, skiing down a great Alpine slope, the snow flying around them while, high in a cobalt blue sky, burnt a scorching sun. He dozed and dreamt. Figures stood below the slope, in the shadow of a ski lift. They were waving. Two figures. And as the boys slid to a halt, Steve could see they were his parents. They wrapped icy arms around him and then he found himself on the chair lift, going up the mountain. Then, over a deep gorge, the lift stopped and, looking down, he saw a busy road. Two people were picnicking in a layby and they waved up at him. It was Mum and Dad. Dad held up a wine glass and toasted him. Dimly, Steve could hear their voices shouting up at him.

'Hello, darling.'

'Hi, Steve.'

Then they got into their car and pulled out. Mum was still waving as the petrol tanker hit them.

4

It was all a bit of an anticlimax when they finally met at the rec. Joe was wearing a dirty old anorak, jeans and trainers and he had an old bag slung over his shoulders. He looked young and afraid, and Kathy suddenly realised that she had brought absolutely nothing with her. Nothing at all. She must be completely mad. Getting away from home had been so important that she had not given a thought to anything else.

They stood by the public loos at the edge of the scruffy park. There were crude graffiti all over the walls. The heat seemed to have increased and she felt dirty and sweaty already. There was nothing dream-like here.

'Where're we going?'

Joe had a kind of pinched look.

'We're going to stay a couple of nights in an old house I know. Then we'll head for Fishguard.'

Despite the pinched look, he seemed very matter-of-fact and oddly confident, and she took heart.

'What old house?'

'Woodenbridge.'

'I'm not going there – that's where the bandstand blew up and . . .'

'It's safe.'

'No.'

'Then I'll go on my own.'

'No.'

Joe looked around him desperately.

'Look, I'm meant to be waiting in my room to go

down the nick with Tim. They'll have missed me already. Come on, I know a short cut.'

Without waiting for her reply, he set off and, after a slight hesitation, Kathy followed him down a dark and murky lane that led towards the council refuse dump. They both sweated profusely as they hurried along and then, quite suddenly, they were out on the tip. Immediately, the foetid smell made Kathy gasp and all she could see were great rising mounds of litter, unidentifiable in its squalid piles. Dust rose behind them as they walked at what seemed like breakneck speed and Kathy suddenly felt lightheaded and unreal. She knew they were walking into danger but she was suddenly too exhausted to care.

Joe knew they would be safe in the sanctuary – safe until he could make up his mind where to go or what to do. He was not in the least upset that he had lied to Kathy about Kerry. Somehow he knew she realised it was only a dream but that dream as much as he did. Joe wanted time to plan and Woodenbridge might give him that time. That Kathy had come at all had both amazed and reassured him. She *must* love him to take part in such a hare-brained scheme. Or was she immature? Or desperate? Or just crazy? Joe became increasingly uneasy as they hurried through the mountains of debris and ever-swarming clouds of flies feasting themselves on the rubbish. One particularly large fly hovered across Kathy's path and for a moment she was sure that its eye held the malevolent gleam of her grandmother's.

Once through the rancid air of the tip, they were out on the heathland. It was tinder dry and dust rose around them as they stumbled along. Between the bracken, sharp and skeletal as it was, ran great runnels, sandy troughs that ravaged the hillsides in uncertain fingers.

Once they crossed the dried-out bed of a stream and, a little later on, a shallow lake that was choked with sand and dead weed. On the higher hills were the fire-raked lands with their skeletal bushes and saplings, and in front of them was a great parched belt of trees that smelt of bitter, acrid, waterless pine. As they moved through it, both felt as if they were walking through a dreadful fairy-tale wood.

They walked on until Kathy felt she would drop, and eventually emerged from the wood on a hillside that overlooked the gaunt chimneys of a verandaed house that was almost smothered in dry scratchy foliage. They stopped and Kathy was surprised to find herself on such high ground, not realising that they had been slowly climbing. Joe was overjoyed. They were here at last and there was no one around. For the moment, at least, they were safe.

'Where are we?' she asked.

'Woodenbridge,' Joe replied.

A chill crept over her. Kathy had never seen such a dump. The house was ugly, with its spotted and overgrown pebble-dashed walls and collapsed veranda. A young sapling had somehow pushed up amongst the rotting wood and there were wild flowers, spiky and thorny, rearing up through the slats. The house was built halfway down the ridge and a knotted jungle of grass and vine and creeper stretched away to a hollow where she thought she saw a glint of reddish water. The water, if it was water, looked oddly out of place. To the left, a wall seemed to run round a patch of darker green and as the land rose again to the right, there was a strip of cracked paving stone, as if a path had once led somewhere.

'Where was the bandstand?' she asked, but Joe brushed her question aside with an impatient shrug.

'I love this place,' he said. 'I often come here.'

'Why?' Her voice was flat now and without expression.

'To get away from people.'

Insects buzzed round the foliage-hung and collapsing front porch and from the walled garden they could see a little black cloud hovering over one side.

'What's that?' she asked.

'There must be some old hives there. That's a swarm of bees come from somewhere else. Escaped from someone else's hive, I suppose.'

There was such a great heat amongst all this desolation that Kathy felt an inward burning, as if something was clawing at her. Almost at once she seemed to have developed a desperate thirst, but when she looked at Joe it disappeared. Suddenly she was without fear or trepidation or any desire to know the future. She wanted to be somewhere with him. Now.

Joe led the way through the brittle grasses round the back of the building and to the back door. Without warning he suddenly darted under the long leaves of an old laburnum hedge. She followed him until they were in a dark tunnel of foliage that seemed to come to a full stop. Joe felt around on the ground, pulled at something and revealed an iron cover. Lifting it with an effort, he indicated a yawning dark gap beneath their feet.

'What's this?' she asked almost eagerly.

'Our hideaway,' he replied quietly. 'No one will find us here, not even Steve.'

She looked at him in sudden fear.

'Does he come here?'

'Yes,' replied Joe quickly. 'He comes to the house.'

'Why?'

'I don't know. He always has. But the main thing is – '

'Well?'

'He never comes to this bit. He doesn't know anything about it.'

'Are you sure?'

'Yes. Come on.'

He led her down an iron ladder that ran the length of the shaft. Little rust granules filtered through her fingers as she gingerly climbed down and then, all of a sudden, they were at the bottom. She could see very little in the gloom but it felt surprisingly cool and hardly musty at all. The place smelt of damp earth and something else – something like candle grease. Then she heard a scraping, hissing sound and saw that Joe had lit a calor gas lamp. He pushed past her, his body smelling of sweat and earth, and the desire in her increased so sharply that she felt a physical pain in her chest.

'I'm just going to close that manhole, then we'll be OK.'

For how long, she wondered instinctively, but for the moment she knew that she did not care.

When Joe returned, he began to pull out the contents of his bag. Kathy eyed his actions and their booty with disappointment. Food and drink were the last things on her mind but, nevertheless, here they were. He lugged out a battered-looking loaf, some cheese, sweaty bits of ham and a flask of water, grey in the half-light. All Kathy could look at were his slim legs and his bare white arms and the beads of perspiration on his forehead.

'What's that?' she snapped and Joe looked at her in surprise.

'They'll be like manna from heaven to you in a few hours' time,' he said, and she suddenly realised that he was sounding much more confident and resourceful than she was. But then Joe was a survivor. 'Or would you prefer to go home?'

She looked at him in amazement. 'Home? What the hell for?'

'Just felt you might be having a few second thoughts.'

She shook her head.

'This won't last us long. It's all I could get. But there's another couple of houses down the hill. One's a holiday home.'

'Well?'

'We'll break in and try to get some more supplies.'

'Break in?'

'We won't get far on this.'

'But if we break in . . .' She suddenly heard her Gran's voice: 'In for a penny – in for a pound.'

They talked in a desultory way for a while.

'I didn't do it.'

'I know you didn't.'

'Steve stitched me up. He put that knife in my room.'

They rambled over old ground until Kathy felt she could bear it no longer. But she knew that she had to go on bearing it because Joe, who had led so well and was proving so resourceful, still needed reassurance, particularly from her. Perhaps he could not believe that she had really wanted to join him, that she would stay with him. After all, he was asking a hell of a lot. Surreptitiously she looked at her watch and knew that he had caught the movement and that it had worried him even more. It was nine o'clock and the sharpness of her desire mounted to unbearable heights.

Perhaps it was looking at her watch like that, that made Joe begin to sense something. The something she wanted. Without warning, he moved closer to her and began to stroke her breasts. Then he buried his face in them and she began to shiver. She had never had sex before, not properly. What was going to happen now? But he drew back and she was amazed to find that she was not as disappointed or as angry as she wanted to be, or thought she would be. They would wait, she suddenly realised, wait for the moment to happen, and that waiting would sustain the whole momentous and terrifying adventure that they were both about to undertake. Despite the dangers, she felt a rising flood of joy. Did he? she wondered. He took her finger and put it to his lips and winked at her.

After a while they ate and Kathy was surprised to find that the food did, after all, taste like manna from heaven. Washed down with the warm tap water, she felt that she had never eaten such a wonderful meal. Then, with feet interlocked, they slept.

Steve tossed and turned, sleep coming in fits and starts. He kept dreaming of his parents, picnicking in the layby, getting back into their car and being torn apart by the petrol tanker. Above all, Steve kept seeing that slender white arm. Waving, waving.

Towards three, he woke and all signs of sleepiness vanished. Steve leant over and reached under his bed. The battered mouth organ he had found in the overgrown garden at Woodenbridge was there. He picked it up and put it to his lips. As usual, no sound came, however hard he blew.

Part Three
ECHOES

I

It was three-fifteen in the morning when Kathy woke, cramped and with a blinding headache. Rather than being fresh and moist in the tiny cellar, or air-raid shelter, or whatever it was, the whole atmosphere seemed to have changed. It was desperately stuffy and the heat inside was unbearable. Kathy felt so miserably claustrophobic that she had to get some fresh air.

She pushed at Joe's feet and pushed at them again, but he seemed unable to wake. She had to give his leg a savage kick before he woke up abruptly, swearing as she had never heard him swear before.

'I've got to get some fresh air,' she hissed at him but he merely grunted at her. When she repeated herself he simply cursed her, but when she tried for a third time he seemed to come to his senses.

'What do you want?'

'I want to get some fresh air. I'm going mad in here.'

'All right.'

He stood up stiffly and she could feel his presence in the almost pitch darkness. Soon she could hear Joe clambering up the iron ladder and then he was whispering for her to join him. She stumbled in the dark, found the rungs and climbed. As he inched open the manhole cover, she felt a rush of clean air, yet with it came something else. They could not believe it. It was the sound of a brass band.

They froze on the ladder, incredulous. Then Joe rammed down the manhole cover again and they were back in the putrid darkness. She could feel him shivering above her and she knew that she was shaking too. Then, with sudden decisiveness, he pushed the cover back and they heard the band again, jauntily playing a tune they could not identify, but which was vaguely familiar. There was another change they had been too shocked to notice before. Daylight was shining down the shaft and they could see bright blue sky.

Before Kathy could stop him, Joe had climbed through the opening and she began to follow more slowly. Then she heard him exclaim very sharply, but all she could see were his trainered feet on top of the shaft.

'What are you doing?' she hissed but he did not reply. She climbed the last few steps towards the sunlight and joined him at the top of the narrow aperture. There was just room for them both.

Kathy could not believe what she saw. But there it was, shimmering below her on a beautiful sunny, yet breezy, spring day. Bunting and flags swirled and the house and grounds were transformed. Smooth lawns fell away to the pine woods and a crisp, white, gravel drive was swarming with cars which looked like something out of a motor museum. Somewhere, she imagined, Steve was playing the mouth organ. He must be – or they wouldn't be here. There was a trim white marquee on the lawns and in and out of this walked smartly dressed men and women. Most of the men were in uniform and the women wore hats and long dresses and carried parasols. To the right of the marquee, a military band played on a well-decorated wrought-iron bandstand in the tea-time light. The house gleamed with new paint and the veranda was set with a long white table that groaned with food. Waiters were going in and out of the house, walking over the gleaming painted slats of the veranda. A long hedge ran round the grounds, with peacocks and other animals shaped out of it. A few white clouds fleeced a cobalt blue sky and they could hear the murmur of conversation and the tinkle of tea cups as the band stopped playing, to a ripple of applause, and then began another, vaguely familiar, number. Kathy suddenly realised it was 'Greensleeves'.

'Blimey!' muttered Joe, and Kathy let out a little whinny of amazement. Then they looked in the other direction, towards the walled garden; because they were so high up they could see neat beds and a fountain. There were beehives nestling up against one of the old walls and above them hovered a swarm of bees, densely packed, a minature black cloud, some seven metres above the hives. No one seemed to notice or remark on them. They just hovered, seemingly without threat or hostility.

'What is this place?' breathed Kathy.

'An old empty house called Woodenbridge,' returned Joe. His voice was like a sigh on the wind.

Empty? What the hell were they seeing? They must still be asleep. They were dreaming, or having a vision, and none of it was real and they would soon wake up. He pinched himself and it hurt. But perhaps he was dreaming the hurt. Meanwhile, the band played on.

There was just enough room for both of them to stand on the top of the ladder and watch. Neither wanted to risk leaving the safety of the manhole cover. Then Kathy froze and for the first time she was afraid, desperately afraid.

'Look.'

Joe looked and at first saw nothing. Then he gasped. On the lawn, walking away from the marquee and towards the bandstand, were Kathy and Steve. Steve was playing his mouth organ.

Kathy watched herself in a state of shock.

'Can you see what I see?' she asked and Joe nodded.

'I can see but I don't believe it.'

Nevertheless, there they were – Kathy in a tea gown and Steve in uniform – and they were walking arm in arm. Then Joe crossed their path and they stopped to chat. Joe was also wearing a very smart army uniform and he looked particularly dashing as he kissed Kathy. Except that – except that they were not *exactly* Kathy and Steve and Joe. Not exactly. They were too tall. Their features were ever so slightly different and they had a new way with them. But not that new. Why, it's as if they are a kind of echo of us, thought Kathy, and Joe decided they were not really them, but people who looked a bit like them. But Steve, the taller, different Steve, had that grin.

Then they went their separate ways. Kathy and Steve, or their echoes, drifted away somewhere behind the bandstand and Joe went into the marquee.

On top of the ladder Joe tried to move but Kathy, by some instinct, grabbed his shoulder and held him back.

'No.'

'Why?'

'I don't know. But don't!'

He sank back and they continued to watch the scene. Nothing much happened, although a lot of people continued to mill about and the band kept on playing. They watched for about half an hour, until they both knew that it was early evening. The band stopped for a while but no one showed any signs of leaving.

Kathy and Joe watched as if in a trance, feeling neither tired nor particularly awake. Then Joe gave a little cry and, when Kathy focussed in the direction he was looking, she saw Steve, or the echo of Steve, beginning to walk slowly towards them. He was grinning Steve's grin but his walk was not Steve's. It was more of a stride, more of a long and loping stride, advancing towards them relentlessly.

'Close the cover,' hissed Kathy as Steve drew nearer, but Joe stood as if hypnotised.

'Close it!' yelled Kathy, tearing at Joe's hands, but he pushed her away and for the first time she really felt how strong he was. She could make no impression on his arms and still Steve kept coming. She could see his grin, hear his feet on the roughening grass, then she could hear him beginning to play his mouth organ. It was 'Greensleeves' – just as the band had played earlier.

'Close the . . .' but, to her absolute horror, Joe did completely the reverse. He drew himself out of the manhole in a quick movement and threw himself at Steve's feet. But directly he had done so, Joe simply disappeared and Steve kept coming, with his mouth organ and marching gait, striding confidently over the very space where Joe had been. Steve was within centimetres of her now and she still stood on the ladder, petrified with fear. Then she knew she had to follow Joe and, without thinking any further, Kathy launched herself out on to the grass and into the sunset.

As she did so, she felt wind and a stinging sensation and Steve disappeared. Instead, she found herself almost lying on top of Joe in the long dry grass of a very dark night. When she looked around her, all she could see was the ruined house; she could smell the hot breathless night and the fire-smitten woods and feel the long grass beneath her. They lay in each other's arms in the foliage and waited for something to happen. But nothing did. The band was silent.

2

They drank in the warm air, shivering slightly at what had happened, but the real unease was deep in the pits of their stomachs. What was happening to them? At school there were blurred images on the TV screen, and out here there were visions and echoes of people. Were they both going mad? And this time the visions were just for the two of them. The more Joe and Kathy thought about the meaning of what they had seen, the more confused and alarmed they became.

'Is it all black magic?' asked Kathy hopelessly but Joe shook his head.

'It's something happening in our minds,' he said. 'Something we don't understand.'

He looked at her shiftily, knowing they were both unsatisfied, then he said: 'You hungry?'

Kathy realised how absolutely starving she was.

'I'm ravenous.'

Joe laughed in the night and his laugh was loving and reassuring. Suddenly she felt a bit better. At least they could share what was happening to them.

'Then we'll have to go exploring.'

'Exploring?'

'Do one of those houses on the other ridge. The empty one.'

'Break in?'

'We're not going to knock at the door, are we?'

'But . . .'

'How hungry *are* you?'

'You know.'

'Then there's nothing to argue about, is there?'

He got up abruptly.

'When are we going to Kerry?'

'Soon.' He sounded irritable and she knew there was nothing more to say. Kathy began to follow Joe's slight figure down the slope towards the river and the next ridge. The night was still and hot and dark and the acrid smell of burnt foliage hung over everything. As they walked through the pine trees, Kathy's exhausted mind tried to connect the images on the TV screen at school, the vague story of soldiers being blown up at Woodenbridge and the full-scale, live-action vision they had just seen. She failed to connect anything at all, but the wrought-iron bandstand haunted her as she plunged on through the pines. Perhaps she *had* gone mad.

Soon they were climbing up again and the air became fresher and purer. Then, almost immediately, they came to a drive that led to a house tucked away into the hill. There was a ragged garden and then the house itself, a bulky shadow, loomed out at them. Joe led the way round the back and she watched him try the windows. It was some time before he managed to find a loose catch, and even longer before he could open the window and insert his lithe body into the narrow gap he had managed to prise open.

'Wait there,' he hissed. 'I'll open the back door.' He disappeared and there was an unbearable delay during which Kathy kept herself going partly by imagining the food they might find and eat, and partly by looking round constantly, sure that there was someone creeping up on her. Suddenly she had the fright of her life, and almost wet herself, as there was a muffled scraping, a hinge screamed like an animal, and a door opened a few centimetres from where she was standing. She must have gasped very loudly because Joe hissed: 'Shut up!'

She went to him, upset that she might have let him down, also knowing full well that she was about to break the law for the first time.

'Come on. There's a load of tinned food and I've found a tin opener. All we have to do is cart away as much as we can.'

She followed him inside, into a huge darkened kitchen where she could make out nothing. But Joe was able to see quite easily and he held her hand in a warm dry grasp to stop her crashing into the littered furniture. At last they came to a larder and began to load things into a plastic bag. When it was full he looked round and found a rather more dilapidated, brown paper bag into which they shoved more tins. In the garden an animal cried out and they both jumped, then there was the purring call of a night jar. The sounds put them on edge and Kathy could see that Joe had lost much of his calm.

They stole out the way they had come and retraced their steps through the pines. The bags were heavy and they often stumbled.

Once Kathy paused and whispered: 'What about drink? We got any drink?'

'I got some cans of fruit juice and there's water in the stream below Woodenbridge.'

'The stream? It'll make us ill,' she protested.

But Joe sounded scornful for the second time that

night when he hissed at her: 'You on a picnic or something?'

After that, she said nothing and followed him dutifully until they came to the stream by Woodenbridge. But as they crossed the gardens Joe suddenly stopped and flung himself on the ground, dragging her down with him. Looking up, she saw what had terrified him. On the opposite hill a chain of lights was slowly moving towards them.

'What are we going to do?' she hissed, but Joe motioned her to silence. Then he beckoned and began to belly-crawl over the grass. She followed him, feeling ungainly, unfit and very afraid. After a few minutes he turned, arched his back and crawled towards her.

'Listen. Once we get off this ridge and we're on the flat, I'm going to make a break for it.'

She shook her head dumbly. It was difficult enough, belly-crawling with a heavy bag of cans, but to run as well? Could she do it?

'You can do it,' said Joe, precisely reading her thoughts and grinning at her in the steamy darkness.

He crawled on for a while and she watched him intently, waiting to see when he was going to make a break for it. Even so, he almost took her by surprise when he suddenly jumped up and began to run as hard as he could. Almost immediately, he gained a long headstart on her as she stumbled to her feet and began to follow him, her breath coming in tiny, fearful, little grunts and gasps.

As Kathy ran, she kept glancing up to see the line of torches. They seemed to be much nearer. Oh God, she sobbed to herself, why did I ever get mixed up with him in the first place? Oh God, why? Her legs seemed to be turning to lead and her breath was now coming so fast that it hurt and she knew she would have to stop any minute. Yes, the torches were coming closer all right and she was sure they were moving faster and faster. Kathy couldn't run much further. They were climbing uphill, the bag was heavier and she was breaking down under the impossible strain of trying to keep up with Joe.

Kathy fell to her knees, the sweat poured down her face and her whole body shook with a grinding fatigue. She must give up. She couldn't go on. But then Joe was beside her, hauling her up.

'Come on. You can do it. We haven't far to go.'

She shook her head hopelessly, but he put an arm around her and, somehow, she was immediately running much more easily. A confidence grew in her. They were going to escape. The bulky shadow of Woodenbridge loomed up. And then, glory of glories, yes, they were there and the manhole cover was almost beneath their feet. Home at last, she thought. Home. It was amazing, but this was home, and the heavy bags of tins were going to ensure that they were self-sufficient. She felt a burst of happiness. Whatever was outside, friend or foe, illusion or reality, they were going to be safe at home, not Kerry, but still home. Suddenly, in her mind's eye, she saw the bandstand. The soldiers were playing 'Greensleeves' and she was standing very near them, so near that she saw one of them wink at her.

3

They were safe. After a meal of cold baked beans, spaghetti, biscuits, fruit juice and corned beef, they both settled down in each other's arms. Gone was Kathy's desire; in it's place was a simple need for comfort. As she dozed off, Kathy thought of what they had seen on the ladder and how mysteriously Woodenbridge had come alive. She thought, too, of their escape as thieves in the night. Then she imagined the coming days and all the dangers they presented. But her main concern was Joe and how they would soon be away from danger, by the sea in Kerry.

Joe lay there, unable to sleep; he had none of Kathy's tranquillity and all he could think of was the enormity of what he had done, of how selfishly he had acted. When he had known that he would have to run, his first and worst thought had been to involve her. Certainly, he needed a companion and she was the only person he wanted, but as Joe lay with his arms round the now sleeping Kathy, he wondered what the hell he was going to do. Surrounded, trapped, and now breaking the law, they had no more chance of getting to Ireland, and the village that didn't exist, than fly. How could he admit it to her? How could he tell her that he had lied? For a while he tried to divert his thoughts, but even the idea of making love to Kathy didn't bite. Before they had run away, he had wanted to so much and had been waiting his opportunity. But now they *had* run away, Joe could think of nothing else but how, in the end, he would have to betray her.

Tomorrow, Joe determined, he would take Kathy

back and give himself up. There was no chance of staying out on probation and he knew that he would go to Detention Centre, or Borstal, or worse. He also knew from other boys how it would be. Because he was small, he would be bullied and beaten up and some of them would make him do things for them that he would not want to do. It was a grisly prospect but he would have to face it sooner or later and he knew that he would have to make it sooner, for later would only extend his punishment and her misery. Mercifully, his mind became consumed by the images of the bandstand, and as Joe drifted into a light, restless sleep, he was sure he could hear the distant strains of a melody: 'Greensleeves'.

4

Joe surfaced from a light doze and imagined he could hear the sighing of waves on a rocky strand. Then, outside, he heard a kind of grinding sound as if a boat was being dragged up a pebble beach. Very carefully, he unwound his arm from Kathy and climbed as silently as he could up the metal ladder. Several times he looked round to see if he had disturbed her, but she was sleeping heavily. When Joe reached the top of the ladder he paused, and then very slowly raised the lid of the manhole. Immediately, he smelt the sea.

The little port was laid out at his feet. Fishing boats were moored up against a small quayside and there was a sharply shelving pebble beach. On top of one of the cliffs was a small cottage or was it a log cabin? Seagulls wheeled behind a returning fishing boat and the air was clear and crisp and smelt of a late spring afternoon, with the scent of some kind of blossom in the light wind that was making the little waves slap at the pebbles in playful style. There was a slight sea mist some metres out, but only a light haze. Joe breathed in the heady aroma and a sense of joy overtook him. Then it left him abruptly, for he knew that if he was to venture outside the sea would disappear. Even to gaze at it from afar was wonderful, but he knew that it would be dangerous to watch for too long, for it gave weight to his lie. Joe climbed the last rungs of the ladder and fell on to the stifling grass of the summer heat. Predictably, his vision vanished, and as he lay sobbing on the dry heathland, he wondered if he could kill himself. Then, from far away, he smelt salt and a solitary seagull suddenly flew across the darkened sky.

Part Four
DUNCAN

I

'You bring it to the door,' said Duncan. 'Reg'll take it from you. Now that old Sandey's out of the way, Reg's taken over at the gate. And he's in my pocket.'

They were talking in a small bus garage in Guildford. It was Saturday morning, so it had been easy for Steve to get away on his own and easier still to stroll unnoticed and unremarked to the bus station near the river. He sat on the bench with his brother, looking as if they were waiting for a bus.

'No one's going to get killed. Little wooden box like that. It'll just break a few windows. Give that bastard Catchpole a shock. And I want to see that.'

'That old man's bad.'

'Sandey? Old pervert. Had it coming to him. But he'll live. Only a few broken bones and a lacerated face.'

'How do you know?'

'It's all over the barracks.'

Steve felt an involuntary shiver course through him. Once again, his mind ran over past events.

★ ★ ★

The tragedy of the Tully family was not confined to Steve's grandfather, Jack. Jack's son had followed his father and grandfather into the army and had been stationed first in Aden and then in Northern Ireland. Later he had been posted to Germany, and it was there that Captain and Mrs Tully had died on the motorway. Steve had been twelve, Duncan twenty-one and already training to be an officer. Steve was shattered when his loving, happy-go-lucky parents had died so suddenly and he had grown to depend totally on Duncan. It was a fatal dependence but there was no one else to rely on. Both his parents were only children and the one grand-parent left, already shattered by her husband's crime and hanging, had been shocked into senility by her son's death and could not look after his children.

So after an unsettled spell in Germany with family friends, Steve was put into the children's home in Camberley when his brother was posted there. He had been there for the last three years and it had hardened him, but he continued to maintain his hero-worshipping dependency on Duncan. But despite his noble looks, Duncan was no hero and ever since his parents' death he, too, had been lost. Together, the family had been strong, but now the children were rootless and all too vulnerable. Steve depended on Duncan and Duncan was losing his identity in a savage world with which he could not cope.

'So it's not a very powerful bomb?' Steve insisted.

'It's only a practical joke.' Duncan grinned, in his hero's way. 'All you do is collect the device from Woodenbridge, and bring it up to Security. After all, you'll be delivering newspapers like you always do.

You'll give Reg the morning paper – and the bomb wrapped up in its little parcel.'

'How does it work?' asked Steve anxiously.

'It's easy.' Duncan's voice began to quicken. 'All you've got in that hidey-hole of yours is a small wooden box with a hole drilled in the side. Bit different from Grandad's day – burning fuses and all that. In our case, there's a big bang. Everyone's scared. No one's hurt.'

Steve didn't like to think of what had happened at Woodenbridge, how his grandfather had died in such disgrace. He knew his family was dogged by tragedy. Fleetingly he wondered if there would now be a third. But Duncan was so confident. Steve tried to control his feelings. Of course there wasn't going to be another tragedy. They had discussed the plan many times, and Duncan had said he relied on him and would take him skiing at Christmas. It was going to be all right. It was just a joke. But what had happened to Mr Sandey wasn't a joke.

'Duncan . . .'

'Yes, old son?' The clean-cut face turned to him with an intimate grin and a strong, reassuring arm was wrapped round Steve's shoulders.

'You said no one's going to get hurt?'

'I told you . . .'

'Mr Sandey . . .'

'Got more than that. But did I do it?' The reassuring grin was still there.

'I did it.'

'You fixed him all right.'

'Too well.' Steve frowned. He felt so confused, but his loyalty to Duncan had always been blind. Tragedy? His life was just one big tragedy and it might as well go on.

Duncan hugged Steve to him. 'I never told you to wreck the whole brake system.'

Steve stared at the ground. 'What did you tell me to do, then?'

'But he's going to be all right,' said Duncan quickly, 'and you laid it on Joe.'

'Yeah.'

'And he's run away.'

'With Kathy.'

Duncan hugged his brother harder and then took his hand away. He lit a cigarette and continued to look like James Bond.

'There's something else,' said Steve.

'Yes?' Instantly Duncan was alert.

Steve found himself looking at Duncan's nails. That was the only feature of his brother that had always worried him: those bitten-down nails. 'I'm wondering if Joe and Kathy are hiding out at Woodenbridge. You know Joe's got a thing about the place.'

'You checked?' Duncan's voice was shrill, but Steve heard it as commanding.

'Yes – and I saw the police searching, too.'

'Then he can't be there.'

'Unless he's got some hidey-hole.'

'You going to check again?'

'Yes.'

'Anything else?' For the first time there was a little break in Duncan's voice.

'One thing: it's all happened before – a bit – hasn't it?'

'Eh?'

'You know the story – Grandad – the bandstand – '

'Oh yeah,' drawled Duncan. 'The bombing. Where the hell do you think I got this idea?'

Duncan laughed quietly and Steve repeated childishly: 'No one's going to get hurt this time, are they, Dunc?'

He laughed loudly this time. 'Of course not.'

There was a long silence. Then Steve said cautiously: 'Why do you hate this bloke so much?'

'Bloke?'

'The bloke you want to scare with this bomb.'

'Catchpole? He's been bullying some of the kids – the squaddies.'

'Oh.'

'I don't like bullies.'

'Why don't *you* bash him?'

'I already did – and got put in the glasshouse for insubordination. So I want to give him a shock. Right?'

'Right.'

'Now, about this skiing trip . . .'

'Yeah!'

'I've made the bookings and we're off to – '

Duncan talked on and all Steve's worries disappeared. It was going to be great in Switzerland. If only Kathy could come with them, he thought, and momentarily he saw himself and Kathy skiing down a vast Alpine slope, to the rapturous applause of thousands. Later they would dance in the moonlight. The master and mistress of Woodenbridge at play.

2

At the end of the third day, Kathy asked: 'When do we go to Kerry?'

Joe, who had been hanging on desperately for nothing, decided now that he would give himself up tomorrow.

'Tomorrow,' he told her and she grinned with joy and flung her arms around him. They had had a very passive and inert two days; in their hideaway during the day, taking a breather on the heath at night. Kathy had slept a lot and they had passed a good deal of time in silence. They had had no rows and at night they had lain in each other's arms while Kathy slept and Joe waited for the sound of the sea on the strand that never came. As a result, he was getting more and more tense, which he took great pains to hide from Kathy. During the day he would make up nostalgic stories of life at Kerry and surprised himself with his inventiveness. But all the time he was fantasising and bringing such happiness to her, he knew that he would soon be put away and that this was probably the last time he would see her. Joe's heart was breaking but he didn't show it, for his fantasies kept him alive, as did the thought of the seagull in the night that might bear him away. There was always that magic and he counted on that hopeless possibility.

For her part, Kathy was very happy and she did not miss home in the least. In fact, she hardly ever thought about it. It was as if she were in a time suspended and that suspension had a good deal to do with the strange feelings she had for Joe, which never came to fruition and yet were still inside her. She waited on his every move. The only other main, and seemingly endless, preoccupation was the vision they had seen. It had not repeated itself. Joe kept trying to persuade her that it was the work of their over-active imaginations, but she wouldn't have that and they came very close to having their first row. Her mind was so totally occupied, she did not detect Joe's increasing tension.

Then, on the third night, he said: 'Kathy, I have to talk to you.'

She looked at him expectantly. 'Is it about Kerry?'

'Yes.'

'About tomorrow morning? About when we start?'

'Mm.'

'Then – '

Joe looked at her grimy face. There was fern in her hair. He was going to have to return her to civilisation. Joe felt hot tears welling up in his eyes. It was like caging a wild bird.

'You see – '

As he spoke, however, there came a noise that riveted them both. A hammering had begun on the manhole cover – a desperate tattoo that sent shards of terror into both their hearts.

'It's the police,' hissed Kathy.

'Or Steve,' whispered Joe, rocking himself to and fro. Then they heard a new sound that was even more terrifying. The manhole cover was being slowly unscrewed.

'Steve.' Joe's voice sounded defeated. Kathy looked up, aghast. This couldn't be happening.

'So this is your hidey-hole.'

'Go to hell,' said Kathy.

'That's not nice,' replied Steve. 'Not nice at all.'

Suddenly his head disappeared and in a few seconds, and with great dexterity, his legs swung through. In a rush, he was standing beside them, panting slightly. His fists were clenched. Instinctively, Kathy made a dash for him but he shoved her aside and she fell to the ground, crying out in pain. Then Joe moved out of the shadows. In his hand he held the sharp kitchen knife that he had stolen with the food.

3

'It couldn't have been Joe – not him.' Mr Sandey raised himself in bed, the alarm spreading over his face. 'Not my Joe.' He flopped back, gasping in pain. Almost completely swathed in plaster, he had two broken legs, a broken arm and severe lacerations to his chest and face. But, for him, all this was nothing to the pain he felt about Joe.

'We found evidence in his room, sir,' said the young police officer, eagerly fingering his pencil and hoping to write down revelatory notes. 'And he's run off.'

'Run off?' Mr Sandey tried to raise himself up again and failed.

'With a girl. A kid of his own age. We've been looking for them for three days.'

'Joe wouldn't have done anything to me. Not to *me*. We're the best of pals. Always have been.'

'Yes, sir.'

'What did you find?'

'A filthy penknife covered with brake fluid. In one of his bedroom drawers.'

'I don't believe it.'

'It was there, sir.'

'It must have been *put* there.'

'Sorry?'

'Put there by somebody else. To make it look as if he did it.'

'Who, sir?'

'Probably that wretched boy Steve. He's always in trouble and he hates little Joe.'

'Why, sir?'

'Because my wife and I have taken an interest in him. He would love to get at Joe and harm me.'

'Why should he want to harm you?' The policeman was so surprised that he forgot to add his usual 'sir'.

'Because I know him all too well. He's an evil boy. Not like my Joe.'

The policeman stood up and closed his notebook with a snap.

'We'll have to look into all this, sir.'

'You must. And find my little Joe. Have you tried Woodenbridge? He used to tell me how much he loved his hidey-hole.'

'The old house. We've been over it dozens of times, sir. They're not there.'

'Are you sure?'

'Positive, sir.'

Of course the bomb was more powerful than he had told Steve it was. But it would disgrace Catchpole and that's what he wanted, whatever the cost. He hoped there would be no cost for, with luck, Catchpole would be court-martialled and that would be the end of him. He would go inside for a good long time.

Duncan had now gone over the plan so many times in his own mind that he knew each step by heart. Steve would deliver the parcel to Reg, who would then place it in the CO's locker. The device would go off when the CO opened the parcel. Everyone knew how disastrous Catchpole's relationship with the CO was and everyone would later know his fingerprints were on the detonator. It hadn't been difficult to organise this. After all, they were both sappers and putting together and taking apart bombs was routine. Duncan had got Catchpole's paw-marks on the detonator with no trouble at all. Of course he feared retribution, but would Catchpole think of him? He had plenty of enemies amongst the other officers and there were quite a few who were capable of this kind of trick. As for Reg, he was going to be given a grand for his trouble, wasn't he? It was worth every penny and, as he distributed the post, he was the only man for the job. Old Sandey was too cautious and would check each parcel. But not Reg, he was only a fill-in, wasn't he? So if they blamed him for being careless, well, it was no skin off his nose.

Getting Sandey out of the way hadn't been very good. But Duncan knew he was an old poof. He'd tried to touch up Steve before he got fixated on Joe, and might try again. So he'd had his just desserts, lucky not to be killed really, and the plan had worked like a dream.

Duncan was timid but manipulative, and ever since his parents' death, he had tried to 'arrange' his life as best he could. He would use anyone, even Steve whom he loved desperately. And now it was Catchpole who was for the high jump.

He lay back on the bed and shut his eyes. Steve had been so strange recently, so much more confident, so much more questioning. Why? Not knowing unsettled him. Slowly, Steve's image disappeared from his mind and he thought instead of his grandfather. They had hanged him for taking revenge. For a while Duncan wondered just what Jack had been up against at the barracks to take such a terrible revenge. Was it as bad as Catchpole?

The door opened suddenly and Catchpole leered his way in.

'Hallo, Dunci, you're looking really upset tonight.'

'Leave me alone.'

'Oh, you wouldn't like to be left alone. Besides, I want company. I've had a bad day.'

'Again?'

'I have a lot of bad days, Dunci. You know why?'

Duncan shook his head.

'Because we have a bastard CO. What is he, Dunci?'

'A bastard CO.'

'And why is Manning a bastard CO?' Catchpole came and sat down on Duncan's bed. The springs shrieked under his weight and Duncan could smell on his breath the curry they had had for supper.

'Because he's nasty to you, Catchpole.'

Catchpole leant over and grabbed Duncan's wrist. He began to twist it.

'Do I detect a bit of winding-up in your voice, Duncan?'

'No.'

'Sure?'

'No!' Duncan screamed out loud in pain as Catchpole gave his wrist another vicious turn.

'OK, then.' He reluctantly released it, clambered off the bed, farted loudly and then plummeted himself down on his own bed. He picked up a copy of the *Beano*. 'This is the life,' he said.

A short one, hoped Duncan.

'Put it down, Joe!'

'Get out!'

'Put it – '

'Go on. Get out, Steve.'

'Not till I've flushed you two out.'

Steve was pacing around Joe and, from the floor, Kathy watched them with alarm. Even with the knife, Joe looked defenceless in front of Steve's bulk.

'Get out of the way!' Joe's soft lilt had menace in it.

It was obvious that Steve sensed this too, as he suddenly hesitated. Then he pounced and she could see his massive hand locked round Joe's thin wrist. Staggering, she got to her feet, but too late, for the knife dropped out of his hand as Joe fell to the ground with Steve on top of him. Steve's hands went for Joe's throat while he kicked and writhed underneath. Kathy leapt on Steve's back, driving her nails into the back of his neck.

They rolled over in a heap in the confined space, knocking aside tins and cutlery and the empty paraffin heater. God knows what would have happened if it had been full, thought Kathy. She didn't have much time to think anything more as they rolled over again.

Steve was too strong for both of them; soon Kathy found herself flung to another side of the sanctuary and she lay there with all the breath knocked out of her. But she had no thought for her own pain as she watched Steve beat Joe senseless.

Catchpole slept, snoring slightly, his mouth half-open. Duncan watched him in creeping panic. For the first time, he did not feel his usual desperate determination to go ahead with his plan, come what may. Instead, he felt apprehension. His sense of reality returned. He must have been crazy. Stirring his brother up to kill a man and get an innocent blamed for it, making Steve hide a bomb and deliver it to Reg, who, no doubt, would prove unreliable and betray him. Suddenly, his magnificent scenario was full of holes – holes that could blow everyone apart. And the whole toppling edifice was just to end Catchpole's bullying. Duncan looked again at his tormentor. Was he really worth it?

But it was too late now. Steve was due to deliver first

thing tomorrow morning. Now there was no going back. Duncan continued to watch the snoring Catchpole, and as he watched the hatred came flooding back. It was strange how hate had all but disappeared. Thankfully, it had now returned and he knew that his intricate plan had been right. Planning was something he had always enjoyed. He loved the preparation and the moment when the well-oiled machinery delivered results. Plan A, Mr Sandey's car, had worked beautifully. Plan B, planting the evidence on Joe, had been equally successful. And Plan C, the most ambitious of all, was to be his most successful, most effective. It must be.

In the past, there had been other plans: how to cope without his parents, how to look after Steve, how to run a little black marketeering in Germany. Everything was calculated towards his own and Steve's survival. And now, all that he'd built up was at stake. For Duncan could not bear to be bullied, could not bear to have the private citadel of his own body abused in the way that Catchpole did it. It was bad enough to have his spirit broken, but to be knocked around so sadistically was unbearable. He looked back at the sleeping Catchpole. It wouldn't be long now. Just twelve hours, to be precise.

Steve stood over Joe, watching him breathe, watching the blood run down his swollen face.

'You bastard,' said Kathy.

'He asked for it.'

'You stitched him up.'

'He fixed Sandey's brakes.'

'Correction. *You* did.'

'How do you know?' Steve turned on her threateningly but in some confusion. This was not the way he had hoped it would be. He had prayed that Kathy would see him as her rescuer.

'I just know you did.'

'That doesn't prove a thing, Kathy.'

'Don't use my name!' She struggled to her feet and walked over to Joe. 'You've killed him.'

'Funny about the breathing, then.'

'He needs a doctor. An ambulance.'

'He'll be fine. No one's going anywhere. Yet.'

'He'll die. Choke on his own vomit.'

Steve said nothing. Taking off his belt, he tied it round Joe's ankles. Joe moaned slightly, but Steve took no notice as he dragged off Joe's belt and used it to tie his hands. Joe moaned again, and then his eyes opened.

'You bastard,' he mouthed.

'Everyone keeps calling me that,' grinned Steve. 'Now, I've got a nice little treat for you.'

'You're going to call the police,' said Kathy bleakly.

'Oh, I am. I might get a reward.' He looked round the floor at the empty cans. 'Looks as if you've been having a thieving spree, as well as going on the run. That'll clock it up a bit. But the police are going to have to wait.'

'Why?' asked Kathy.

'Because,' said Steve. 'Just because.'

'Wait for how long?' rasped Joe.

'A few hours.' Steve paused and grinned again. 'You see – we're going to spend the night together. That's nice, isn't it?' He pulled something out of his back pocket. It was the battered mouth organ. 'Anyone like a tune?' he asked softly. He looked very confident – almost as if he were controlling them.

'Are you crazy?' wept Kathy.

But Steve didn't play right away. He just held the mouth organ to his lips, grinned in his old truculent way, then put the instrument down on the earth floor of the sanctuary. It was as if he were challenging them, thought Kathy. But to what?

'Where did you get that thing?'

'I found it in an old beehive, stuck right at the back.'

'Why were you looking in an old beehive?'

'For a hiding place.' The words just slipped out before he could help it.

'What for?'

'None of your business.'

Kathy wanted to keep him talking, for while Steve was talking, he wasn't dangerous. It was when he stopped and silently played the mouth organ that things began to happen.

'Steve.'

'Mm?'

'What happens when you play that?'

Steve didn't grin this time but merely picked up the mouth organ. He put it to his lips and put it down again. Kathy realised she was sweating, but she didn't think he was teasing her this time. Steve seemed to have a genuine reluctance to play the mouth organ. Why? she wondered. Why? And Joe, whose mind was clearing rapidly, wondered the same as he strained hopelessly at his bonds. Then Steve looked directly at Kathy for the first time since he had arrived and she stared back at him, shocked and bewildered. She had never seen such a look on Steve's face before. It was a look of fear.

'What's the matter?'

'Nothing.'

'There *is* something. Tell me.'

'Nothing.'

'*Tell me*.' She was standing a few centimetres away from him and she could detect that the need to tell was very great indeed – so great that he didn't mind Joe there, listening, absorbing.

The words came out in a rush. 'When I found it – the thing didn't make any sound. But I saw things.'

'Like we *all* saw things?'

'Yes, but I never saw nothing . . . personal.'

'You mean, you never saw anyone close to you near that bandstand?'

'And you never saw yourself, but not quite yourself?' said Joe.

Steve turned on him immediately. 'You shut up for a start, or I'll do you again.'

'Go on,' said Kathy, making her voice warm. 'Go on.'

'I played it again. Just now. While I was walking about the grounds.'

'What did you see?'

'I saw my dad and mum. They're dead.'

'How?'

'I saw the car. It was here.'

'*Here*?'

'Just by the trees. It was on its side – all smashed up. And Dad and Mum – they were all smashed up, too.' His voice broke.

'What else did you see?' Kathy knew there was more to come.

'I saw this bloke. Pushing up the manhole cover. Coming out. Walking over to them. Laughing and carrying on.'

'Carrying on?'

'Like he was celebrating.'

'Who was he?'

'He looked like me.' Steve's voice broke again and she

could see the frightened tears in his eyes. 'I think he was my grandfather.'

'Who?' Joe and Kathy's voices were raised in unison.

'This place belonged to my great-grandparents. It was my grandfather, guy called Jack, who blew up the soldiers. He had a grudge against one of them.'

'So he blew them all up,' said Joe bleakly.

'He didn't care.'

'No,' said Kathy. 'He couldn't have done.'

'They say, my dad said, that Jack could hate. He could really hate. It was a family thing. He said we were all good haters.'

'What about your grandmother?'

'She was pregnant, with my dad, when Jack was nicked. He was hanged. And this is *his* mouth organ, all right. It said in the paper, he was playing it to the bees when the soldiers came to get him.'

Joe stifled a laugh and Steve swung round on him, kicking him in the side.

'For God's sake – '

'I told him to shut up.'

As Joe sobbed with pain, Kathy again heard Steve's words: 'It was a family thing. He said we were all good haters.'

'What do you mean?' she asked, as gently as she could. 'What do you mean about the bees?'

'It's another family thing.'

'Yes?'

'We tell it to the bees. It's an old custom. Dad used to keep bees wherever we were, even if we were on a short-duty spell. He had bees in Aden, bees in Germany, bees in Chester. Bees everywhere. And if he had a problem, he'd tell it to the bees. Grandfather did, he said. But he used to play music to them, too.'

'On the mouth organ?'

'S'pose so.'

'What do you think the mouth organ does? Why does it make pictures?'

'I don't know.' The whole idea seemed to floor Steve.

Not so Joe. 'It must be the hate,' he said slowly and viciously, struggling to breathe, and Steve listened, too surprised or stupefied to shut him up.

'What are you talking about?'

'Hate's powerful,' said Joe. Silently Kathy agreed, thinking of her feeling for her gran. Hate was *very* powerful.

It was just after six when the police moved slowly up the rutted and overgrown drive to Woodenbridge. There were three cars, two vans – full of dogs and their handlers – plus another van, full of uniformed constables. 'One last look,' they had been told. 'One last, very intensive look.' Directly the convoy arrived in front of the house, policemen and dogs poured out. It was still early on in the July evening and there would be enough light for at least another couple of hours. Anyway, if they didn't finish, they could always come back tomorrow.

There had been so many times over the last few days when Kathy had been afraid, but at no time had she been as afraid as she was now. She shivered and sweated at the same time, as Steve's words ran round and round in her head. The hatred – it was so strong. Steve's grandfather. And Steve. For now he was looking at Joe – and the hatred was there. He walked over to him and put his hands round his neck.

'What are you doing?' asked Kathy. 'What *are* you doing?' She forced the words out. But he didn't reply and went on squeezing Joe's neck until she could see the veins standing out in his thick podgy hands and the blueness pouring into Joe's face. His tongue flopped out and he looked absurd, like a doll someone was breaking up. Kathy remembered a boy tearing an arm off her teddy bear. It was like that. And always the words going on in her mind. The hatred.

Then reality came back and Kathy screamed aloud as Joe's tongue lolled around his chin and Steve went on squeezing, squeezing until Joe's neck was just one big red weal.

'Was that a scream?' asked one of the policemen as they walked in line across the ragged landscape. They all stopped and listened. There was no repetition, and most of them had heard nothing. As they walked slowly on, scanning the ground, even the policeman who had heard Kathy decided that he had been mistaken.

She hurled herself on Steve's back, pounding and tearing at him. But it was like riding some strong animal; he tossed her off in seconds. She climbed back and he tossed her off again and so it went on, this hopeless, unequal combat, until she was too bruised and too exhausted to attack him again. As Kathy lay breathless on the ground, she saw the mouth organ beside her. With her last remaining strength she picked it up and blew into it. As she did so, music filled the room. A military band was playing 'Greensleeves'. Slowly, Steve took his hands away from Joe's neck.

The Greensleeves tune was muffled and Kathy looked round, expecting to see something but not knowing what it would be. For a while she saw nothing, until she heard the cry of fear from Steve.

'It's Grandfather.'

There were two Steves in the room. One was the Steve she knew, crouched, watching, pointing, his lips parted in fear. The other was another Steve. He looked like him, but wasn't. It was Jack and he was assembling something. His fingers moved deftly; clearly, he knew what he was doing. He packed powder into a canister and then attached a fuse. The work was slow, cautious, above all conscientious. But it was his eyes she watched. The hatred was in them, so strong that it was a force that radiated savagely about him.

They watched him for what seemed like hours, not daring to move. Then he got up, a shadow, an echo that was not part of their time, but was very much a part of them. Her hatred for Gran, Steve's hatred for Joe, Jack's hatred for a colleague, and God knows who else's hatred spiralling up and around them.

With a little grunt of satisfaction, Jack passed them and silently began to climb up the shaft. There was a rush of air as he raised the manhole cover and then he passed on. Kathy found she still had the mouth organ to her lips and that she couldn't put it down, try as she would. Then she stared down at Joe and knew he was dead. Trembling, she looked up at Steve and saw he was grinning. But then Jack had been too, she realised. And the grins were identical.

The police had given up for the night and were leaving, having resolved to return tomorrow. The convoy filed slowly down the overgrown drive into the setting sun and was silhouetted on the edge of the hill in its last golden fiery rays. They disappeared into the twilight, leaving Woodenbridge to its past and the continuing force of hatred.

* * *

'He's dead.'

'So will you be, if you don't come with me.'

She backed away, terrified. 'Where are we going?'

'We're going to listen to the band.'

It was such a beautiful summer's afternoon and Woodenbridge was looking its best. Kathy and Steve walked the smooth lawns. She was wearing a long print dress and carrying a parasol. On her head she wore a very heavy, very floral hat. But despite this, she felt confidence in her appearance, knew that the milling crowd were looking at her and commenting favourably. Still the band played 'Greensleeves'. Didn't they know any other tune?

Beside her, Steve looked very dashing in his bright brocaded officer's uniform. His narrow trousers, polished shoes and red tunic suited him beautifully and she no longer hated him. Indeed, she felt very proud and fond of him as they strolled along, arm in arm. Then she looked at Joe in the band. He wore an almost identical uniform but with a different kind of hat. Perhaps it was a bandsman's hat – she really wasn't very clear. He was playing the flute and his eyes were closed as he played. The dark sunlight lit his throat and she could see a red weal. She gasped, but then she saw it wasn't a red weal after all – it was his red tunic, buttoned so close to his chin. Her heart soared. I love you, I love you, she thought, and then she knew, as she hung on to Jack's arm, to Steve's arm, to whose? She knew about Jack now. Poor old Jack. She – whoever she was – she was unfaithful to him. So he had even more reason to hate his brother officers. Whatever happened between them at the barracks might have been bad enough. But what she was doing to him at home was awful. And now, as she clung to his arm, she knew – and she could feel his hatred – and his pleasure. She looked at Joe – or whoever he had been – playing away, his eyes closed. Perhaps he was thinking of her while he was playing.

They strolled on and she could feel the strength of Jack's arm through his tunic. Why was she doing all this to him? He was a good husband and his family were rich and successful. They would have Woodenbridge when his father died – and *they* would be rich and successful. And then there was Edward – who had nothing and would achieve nothing. But she loved him – oh, how much she loved him. Sometimes she wondered if Jack knew, for she had heard that he and Edward didn't get on at the barracks. She also knew how much Jack hated the army now, but his parents didn't want him to leave and wouldn't buy him out. So he was stuck, hating the army, hating Edward. But not hating Edward for her. For surely he didn't know. *Surely* he didn't.

'Come on, Rosie, let's have some tea.'

'It'll be a terrible crush.'

'It's a long way from the bandstand. Come on.'

'Don't you like the band?'

'This is the fourth time they've played "Greensleeves". I find their repertoire a bit limited, old girl.'

He propelled her firmly away, nodding to acquaintances while she smiled brightly, artificially. The four o'clock heat was fierce now and there was a smell of crushed grass and canvas. Woodenbridge, rearing up above them in its rackety way, was resplendent in a coat of new white paint and the lawns were mown like green velvet. Roses bloomed in the flower-beds below the house and the soldiers' uniforms were brilliant as they moved about the grounds. The gravelled paths had been swept and there was bunting everywhere.

'Hallo!' She paused, looking towards the walled garden.

'Come on, darling. We'll miss the strawberries.' He was tugging at her now, very urgently.

'No, wait.'

'Come *on*.'

'Jack – you're hurting me. Why on earth are you in such a hurry?'

'I'm hungry.'

'But look – '

Now he had paused and was following her eyes. A little black cloud hovered over the garden.

'Bees,' he said. 'A swarm. I'll have to see to that later.'

'Someone's been telling the bees.' She smiled at him but he only frowned and she saw there were beads of sweat on his forehead.

'What on earth's the matter, Jack?'

'Nothing. We must get to that tent.'

'*Must*? You're hurting. What's the matter?'

'Shut up!'

'What?'

'Shut up.' He was snarling at her like a frightened animal. 'Will you come – or shall I drag you?'

'Why – ' He seized her arm and literally pulled her along. Then it came. A great rush of hot air. Confused sounds. Silence. And she and Jack were in the grass. At least, she was and he was on top of her. She smelt burning and something else. Something acrid. She pushed him off her and rolled over. The bandstand had gone. In its place was a great sheet of rolling black smoke. People were lying on the grass. One man was rolling towards her. He had no legs.

* * *

It was over. She was holding Joe's head in the sanctuary, cradling it in her lap. Steve was standing by the shaft, leaning on the ladder. He looked as if he had been crying.

Part Five
JACK

I

'We have to get him to a doctor, Steve.'

'He goes nowhere.'

'I thought he was dead.'

'I hoped he was – until you found a pulse.'

'It's weak.'

'He'll live.'

'Please . . .'

'No.'

'I'll do anything for you, Steve. Anything.'

'Marry me?'

'Eh?'

'If I get him to a doctor – will you marry me?'

'We're still at school.'

'Then we'll be engaged. Until we're old enough to be married.'

He was grinning again and she was exhausted. Had she really walked with him over smooth green lawns? Or who *had* she walked with that was so like him, so like her? And what had happened to Joe, or someone like him, blown up on a bandstand? Or strangled by Steve? There were visions and echoes and reality, and it was all horribly mixed up.

But none of that mattered. It was only important to get Joe to a doctor. Now. If he did that, she would agree to anything Steve wanted, however outrageous.

'Yes!'

'You'll marry me if I get him to a doctor?'

'Steve – '

'Or he can stay and bloody rot here.'

'Steve – '

'What is it to be?'

'Yes.' She nodded hopelessly. 'Yes.'

'You'll marry me?'

'I'll marry you.'

'You promise?' His grin had gone and his podgy face was full of joy.

'I promise.'

'Cross your heart – '

'And hope to die.'

'Will you kiss me? Seal it – with a loving kiss?'

'All right – and then – then you'll help me get Joe to a hospital?'

'Yes.'

Kathy laid Joe tenderly on the floor and stood up.

Steve took a couple of steps towards her and she hesitated.

'Do you find me so horrible?' His voice was quiet, humble.

But she felt nothing. She pursed her lips. 'Kiss me,' she said and threw back her head. His lips were cool and firm.

Steve lay with his head on Kathy's lap, like a very young child who was afraid of some future event. Kathy stroked his hair and Steve closed his eyes. Then, a few minutes later, he struggled slowly to his feet and asked her to help him. Somehow they managed to drag Joe up the ladder. He flopped about so limply that Kathy was sure that if he were not dead now, he soon would be. Occasionally he grunted and gasped and moaned. All tiny sounds; all of them frightening to hear. But Steve was even stronger than Kathy had imagined, and soon he had pushed the manhole cover back and they were out in the moonlight.

For a moment they both stood panting over Joe while he lay prone on the ground.

'The hospital's a couple of miles away,' said Kathy. 'How do we get him there?'

Steve smiled – the grin had really gone, defeated by a good smile, full of strength. 'I'll carry him down to the road. Then we'll have a joyride.'

'Joyride?'

Steve smiled in the new way, reassuring and almost apologetic. 'We're going to have to nick a car and get him up there in that. Then we'll dump the car and come back here.'

'Back here?'

'It's all part of the bargain.'

But the bargain seemed to be increasing all the time. What more would he want? And why did he want her back at Woodenbridge? As if to answer her question, Steve said gently: 'I'm going to hide you till mid-morning.'

'Why?'

'I have to do something – run an errand.'

'And then?'

'I'll come back and fetch you.'

'And take me home?'

'No way.'

'Then what?' She looked at him in bewilderment and gathering fear. Was he crazy?

'If you can be persuaded to run away with the likes of him, then you can come with the likes of me.'

'Run away?' She stared at him. Perhaps he *was* mad. Suddenly she thought of Joe's village and yearned for it. If she could save Joe's life, that's where they would end up. Nothing could stop them being together. But if she didn't go along with Steve, then Joe would surely die.

'Where are we going?' she asked wearily.

'You're coming skiing,' he said. 'My brother's taking me.'

'I can't ski.'

'Neither can I.'

There was something funny about his voice, and when she looked into his eyes she could see that there were tears in them again. No, she decided, Steve wasn't mad. He was driven. Desperate. As desperate as Joe had been when he had first phoned and got her to go to Woodenbridge. There was nothing for it, she would have to go along with him, for going along with Steve was Joe's only chance.

Once again Kathy wondered at Steve's physical strength as he carried Joe. In the stark moonlight they could pick out the presence of new car tracks on the sandy soil, and they were silent for they knew that the search was still going on and even now, at almost ten o'clock, they were not safe.

All at once they were in the streets. Just a little further down from Woodenbridge there was a network of wide avenues where big houses were set back in the pine trees. There was a leafy musky scent to the air and Kathy suddenly found it refreshing to be away from the burnt-out hillsides and the awesome claustrophobia of the sanctuary.

Steve put down Joe's body as gently as he would have put down a kitten and then turned to Kathy.

'Stay with him while I find a car. I shan't be more than a few minutes.' He sounded both reassuring and matter of fact.

He darted off into the darkness and Kathy turned to Joe. He was breathing lightly but the weal on his neck looked even more livid and raw in the moonlight. She took his hand and he opened his eyes. She could hardly bear to watch the pain in them.

'You're going to be all right,' she said. 'You can rest soon.'

He closed his eyes without replying, and for a ghastly moment she thought he was dead. Desperately, she searched for his pulse and found it after a struggle. It was faint but regular and she breathed such a loud sigh of relief that she was afraid someone would come. But no one did. Then she heard the sound of a car engine and started back into the hedge. A huge Mercedes was backing down towards them.

The Mercedes stopped beside her and Steve's brutish head poked out of the window.

'OK?'

'Yeah.'

'Right.'

He sprang out and grabbed Joe's arms, half-carrying, half-dragging him into the back seat. When he had shut the door, he opened the passenger door and urged her to jump in 'bloody snappy'.

Kathy did as she was told and clambered in beside him. Steve let the clutch out and the Mercedes glided into life. There was hardly any engine noise as they nosed down the tree-lined road. The moon rode high above them and Kathy suddenly relaxed. She was caught up in the most dangerous situation of her life and was also having terrible difficulty in sorting out reality from illusion in all these living echoes of the past of which they were now part. Yet Kathy felt inexplicably confident as they glided slowly through the empty streets, and it only seemed a few seconds before they were pulling up in the deserted hospital car park.

'Come on.'

Steve got out, opened the back door and gently carried out Joe. He was still breathing, for Kathy could see the rise and fall of his slim chest as it nestled in Steve's strong arms. She followed them to Casualty, and although she knew she could run away now, go home out of trouble, Kathy couldn't leave. Steve's presence was too big, too powerful. They stopped at the door and Steve gently put Joe down just outside it. Then he rang the bell hard, grabbed Kathy's hand and began to run as fast as he could, dragging her towards the Mercedes. Once inside, he revved the engine gently and they turned in a tight circle. There was no screech of tyres as they made their getaway, but nevertheless Kathy could see the lights of the police car as it drew in behind them. A second later Steve saw them too; he suddenly gunned the accelerator and the big car leapt forward in a smooth rush of speed. As they did so, the police car began to sound its siren relentlessly.

'We'll outrun them,' said Steve with quiet confidence.

Kathy sat there rigid as the Mercedes sped on. The inside was so posh that she hardly dared lean her head back. What would happen if Steve crashed the car? They'd be in even greater trouble. Perhaps they would die. Suddenly Kathy came out of her trance; she was now so terrified that she began to emit a kind of wail.

'Shut up,' snapped Steve and with amazing dexterity

he leant over and slapped her hard round the face. As he did so, he still somehow managed to keep control of the car.

After Steve had hit her Kathy no longer wanted to cry out. She sat and shivered violently as the police siren seemed to shrill even more urgently than before. But they were not gaining and, when Kathy dared to look out of the window, she could see that the police car had receded a little. But now it was beginning to rain and they were heading for the lights of the town. Great patches of white light, reflected off the puddles and oncoming headlights, continually dazzled her, and the strips of neon threw fluorescent light into the kaleidoscope of colour. Gradually, they were coming out on the other side of town and heading back towards the safety of Woodenbridge. Safety? Kathy wondered how she could ever think of Woodenbridge as a place of safety after all that had happened there.

Just as they were nearing the hill, another police car suddenly shot out of a side turning with its lights blazing and siren wailing. Meanwhile, the car behind began to gain on them.

'OK,' said Steve and yanked at the steering wheel. With a screaming of brakes and tyres, he somehow managed to drag the Mercedes into a sharp turn, and for a moment Kathy wondered if they were going to overturn as they careered round the corner and on to an unmade road. The pot-holes seemed enormous as the car plunged this way and that, but Kathy had eyes only for what was going on behind. With a cry partly of joy, partly of amazement, she saw the police cars roar past the end of the road and then heard the screech of their brakes as they came to a dead halt. She heard them revving up and reversing, but the Mercedes ploughed on until there was no more road and they were roaring across a clearing in the woods.

Steve slammed on the brakes and yelled: 'We must leave the car. Come on.'

As she scrambled out, Kathy heard the police car sirens again as they tore down the unmade road towards them, bumping and swaying as they hit the pot-holes.

They ran side by side towards the hillside, then Steve grabbed her hand, just as Joe had done a few days before. It was amazing; she was being pursued again, running once more towards Woodenbridge at night. Kathy heard the slamming of doors behind her, but they were running up a little gully and, with Steve's hand on her arm, just like Joe's, Kathy suddenly felt that she could go on running forever. Scrambling up the top of the gully, they came to a ridge that ran up the hillside and she knew that in the next valley lay the sanctuary of Woodenbridge. It was the only refuge they had. A dream house. Their dream palace. The rain had stopped now and it was a clear night. She could no longer smell the burnt-out landscape; all she could smell now was a clean pine fragrance as they ran on. It was as if something was helping them along – some force – for now the policemen were stumbling along some hundred metres behind them and, with every step they took, it seemed that they were leaving the police increasingly behind.

I thought it was a force of hatred. The words kept going through Kathy's mind. Then she thought of Steve and how she had hated him, but now he was protecting her, giving her feet wings. Love and hate were so near that, perhaps, they were almost one.

As they approached the Woodenbridge drive, Steve guided her far to the left until they were heading deep into the pine woods.

'Where are we going?' She was not even breathless and felt that she could run on forever.

'We're going to shake them off in the woods. I don't want them to think we're at Woodenbridge.'

With that, he took her hand again and they ran lightly on. Behind them, the policemen cursed and blundered, but after a while Kathy could no longer hear or see them. A little breeze had sprung up in the rustling woodlands and it was as if they were being carried along on its wings. Their feet made no sound and the air in Kathy's lungs ran free and clear. She had never been so happy in her life. Steve's hand was strong and sure and she had now quite forgotten all the terrible things that he had done to Joe. She had forgotten Joe completely.

Doubling back on themselves, Kathy and Steve crept cautiously across the lawns of Woodenbridge and then raced silently for the manhole cover of the sanctuary. Once inside, they lay in the cool dark space, panting and wallowing in the safety they felt. The police had searched Woodenbridge three times now and would no doubt return early tomorrow morning. But even then, they were both sure that they would not find the sanctuary. It seemed untouchable; even the sniffer dogs wouldn't find them. Kathy, too, was untouchable, thought Steve. Somehow he knew, if he even so much as put his arm round her, the spell would be broken.

'Anything to eat?'

'Baked beans and sardines and stale bread. After that, we're out.'

'We won't need it.'

'Where are we going?' Kathy asked but she wasn't worrying. She was safe, safe.

'*You're* going nowhere.'

Even this sinister comment didn't deter her. Kathy

felt completely relaxed. After a while they ate slowly and even the stale bread tasted wonderful.

'Why did you do all that to Joe?' Kathy was surprised by her own calm. Maybe Joe was dead. She felt she was sliding away from the present. Nothing seemed to matter. Suddenly she looked at Steve and saw, for a flash of a second, that he was wearing army uniform. A bright red tunic. Then it was gone and he was saying: 'I've always hated him.'

'But why?'

'Because he came here. This is my house. This is all I've got.'

'But it's *not* yours.'

'It should be,' he said fiercely, 'and he came interfering. He came messing about – '

'P'raps he saw it as *his* home.'

'It radiates home,' said Steve and for a moment she was jerked back to the past. His voice was different. The voice of someone else. Then he spoke as Steve again: 'It's like it casts a spell.'

It has, thought Kathy. It *has* cast a spell. We're all in Woodenbridge's power. Even Joe in the hospital.

Steve looked at his watch. 'Past midnight,' he said. 'Got to do my newspaper round at six.'

'Won't they be looking for you?' But she didn't really care, although she didn't hate him any longer. She was drawn to him now.

'They didn't catch sight of my face in that car. If I don't go back, then they *will* suss me out.'

'Should we sleep then?'

'We could. Maybe we should. But I'd rather we didn't.'

'Then what?'

'I want to show you round the house, Rosie.'

'Eh?' His voice was different again. Steve pulled the mouth organ out of his pocket and breathed into it. Above them Kathy heard the chatter of birds and what sounded like a veteran car. She was startled to find the sanctuary was full of early morning summer light; the manhole cover was open. Moving to the bottom of the shaft, Kathy saw the clarity of a rain-washed sparkling blue sky.

I wonder if I'm asleep? thought Kathy as she wandered across the trim lawns of Woodenbridge. Her watch showed past midnight but she knew it was early morning. She wore a skirt and jumper and there were pearls at her throat. Steve was wearing a sports jacket and wide flannel trousers and a check shirt with a regimental tie. On the carefully raked drive stood an Alvis sports car. It was green and black and its long bonnet gleamed.

'Rosie – '

She turned at the name, recognising it, accepting it with easy familiarity, yet knowing at the same time that it was not her. Just an echo.

'Yes, Jack?'

'We'll go for a spin after breakfast.'

'Where to?'

'Guildford way? We could stop at a roadhouse for lunch.'

'That would be lovely.'

Arm in arm, they went into the house. The interior was magnificent and the rooms were furnished with chintzy chairs and sofas, Persian carpets and landscapes that looked like Scotland. There were also dozens of photographs: family groups and portraits. Kathy recognised them comfortably without really knowing them. Each room was painted in a beautiful white-cream and in the hall and on the stairway there were lightly gilded ceilings and carpets as deep and as springy as lush grass. Their feet made no sound; it was like a slow version of last night's running, for Kathy seemed to have no contact with the ground. Eventually they arrived in the breakfast room where there was a delicious smell of fried bacon and fresh bread. Sunlight streamed through the mullioned windows and dappled the pure white cloth with its clutter of bone china. There were fresh flowers in the centre of the table and little castles of butter, pristine and covered in tiny drops of water. Behind the sunlit table was a sideboard loaded with breakfast dishes: bacon, scrambled eggs, fried bread, kidneys, kedgeree, kippers, a joint of cold beef, melon, ham –

'Let's tuck in,' said Jack.

'Let's,' replied Rosie.

'Yes, that's Joseph Marney.'

'He has severe contusions to the throat and lacerations on the face. Considerable bruising to the body. He was literally dumped on the doorstep a couple of hours ago. And I gather there's been a police chase since then.'

'Yes,' said Tim, digesting the information. The police had already been at Rivermere and Steve's absence had been noted. He felt completely bewildered. Suddenly, mayhem had broken out and he was unable to do anything about it. 'Is he going to pull through all right?'

'Oh, yes. The throat's the worst mess. He could be out in a couple of days, but he's going to be very sore.'

'Is he conscious?'

'Conscious and hungry. But we've told him he won't be able to swallow anything but liquids for a couple of days. We've given him some Complan.'

'Can he talk?'

'That's what the police asked. And he can't. But I'm sure he'd be pleased to see you.'

Almost immediately Tim felt his spirits rising, for he had feared the worst.

'Can I see him now?'

'Sure. But don't stay long.'

The doctor led Tim down the corridor and into a side ward. Joe lay there, almost unrecognisable. His face was black and blue and heavily swollen, while his eyes were mere dark slits. There was surgical lint at his throat, but the slits were open and questioning as Tim came towards him. He spoke, his voice a hoarse whisper.

'He stitched me up. You know that. You know that, don't you?'

Tim nodded.

'He did this to me. All this.'

'Don't talk, old son.' Tim went to the bed and sat on it and took Joe's hand. But Joe dragged it away.

'He's barmy,' Joe rasped. 'You know he's barmy, don't you?'

The food tasted very distant in her mouth – not a taste at all really, more like an echo of a taste. And they didn't talk – or at least she thought they did, but she couldn't hear it. After a while they left the table and walked back through the hallway, passing an umbrella stand. It was full of walking sticks and each one had a snake's head. They passed a table with letters on it and then went out underneath a carved wooden sign that said 'Bless This House'. Outside on the gravel stood the Alvis.

The police convoy returned to Woodenbridge at 3 a.m., reinforced with spotlights and a large number of dogs. They also brought with them a caravan with the words

MOBILE POLICE INCIDENT CONTROL ROOM painted on its side. From inside, radios crackled and the screen of a word processor radiated its green light. The search of the house and grounds had begun again and this time there were treble the number of officers. There was a general determination not to leave any part of Woodenbridge unsearched.

There was no engine noise and the Alvis seemed to float through a hazy, shadowy world that was sometimes brightly lit – the summer day breaking dramatically into a far more indistinct world. Jack drove her through an English landscape of country lanes, high-banked hedged fields and villages. Occasionally they passed another vehicle, once an old Austin van and, again, a tractor and haycart. But it was as if this was a gauze, for, reflected behind the spire of a village church, she saw soldiers huddled in muddy trenches and a great field of pitted loam with shell-torn trees, broken and jagged, sentinels on its edge. In a duckpond she saw soldiers reflected, moving through a shattered forest, and in a field of shimmering wheat she saw a ruined village, full of craters and burnt-out homes. What was she seeing? A marching band walked out of a village school, their uniforms bright and fresh and clear-cut in the drifting landscape. Once she heard church bells, but they were confused by the sound of heavy guns firing nearby. She smelt wild flowers and cordite, hayfields and burning wood, pine trees and the sweet and terrible stench of death.

Then the Alvis came to a stop by a hazy quiet meadow that seemed locked in a gloom which was occasionally irradiated by sunbeams. Hand in hand, they crossed the grass that was covered in frost, except where the sun-beams struck it, and then it was covered in daisies, heads up to the teasing sun. Eventually they came to a river, and at first it looked green and translucent with a light mist playing on its surface. But then it changed from underneath, and the redness frothed up and the current became stronger and the river was filled with blood.

'Where are you going, Rosie? Rosie? Rosie? Rosie?' The words resonated and then stopped, as if plugged by some woolly dampness. She was running across the frost, away from him, until she reached another shaft of sunlight. She stood in it and it warmed her. Then she heard the sound of the mouth organ – 'Greensleeves' – and the sunbeam faded away.

Kathy ran on until she turned a corner, a bend in the river, and suddenly she found herself running on sand dunes. The river was no longer there, but in front of her was a harbour, a jetty and, turning, she saw a small wooden cabin breathing smoke into a sky full of puffy clouds, racing against pale blue. The sun shone steadily on the dunes, casting her shadow into someone else's. Someone else who was standing barefoot beside her. Joe. He took her in his arms and they fell on to the sand, his lithe light weight on top of her. She was home.

Kathy woke, calling out Joe's name. The space around her was cold and bleak, and when she opened her eyes she saw only a squalid cave with its floor littered with refuse. There was a nasty stuffy smell in her nostrils. Of Steve, there was no sign. Instead of feeling safe and distanced from reality, Kathy felt a yawning fear. She was shivering with cold and the calor gas light was flickering low. She knew that there was no more gas and that soon she would be in a cold darkness. She rose stiffly to her feet. She had decided to push up the manhole cover and give herself up to the police. At least she would learn about Joe and how he was. Now her feelings were reversed. She needed Joe desperately and all her old powerful feelings of love had returned. But what had not returned was her original hatred of Steve. Instead, she felt a vague affection for him, a shadowy understanding. Then she saw the piece of paper crammed into a flat sardine tin. It was oily and smelly and when she picked it up and unscrewed it she could barely make out the pencil scrawl. Then, slowly, she began to decipher it.

Dear Kathy,
I'm going to try and get past the police. I bet they are here already. They'd be fools if they weren't. Anyway, I know a back way out and I'll chance my luck. I'm going back to the home to pick up my bike. I have to run an errand for my brother. It's very important. When I get back, I'm going down the nick. I want to get that little bastard off the hook about Sandey, and then they'll do me for beating him up. I expect that they will put me away for a long time, so I don't know when I'll see you next.

I do love you, Kathy. I always have and that's what made me do all the bad things. I'll miss the skiing but it doesn't matter that much. At least we had a night together. It was good, wasn't it, Kathy? Say it was good.

Steve.

Steve had made it. At least so far. He had managed to belly-crawl out of Woodenbridge and make his way down a series of glades and over the countryside without alerting the attention of the police. It had been quite a miracle, and he wondered if he was bearing a charmed life for some purpose or other. The luck held at Rivermere. There was no one about and the bicycle shed was unlocked. He brought out his bike and, as silently as he could, he cycled away. He had retrieved the package from its dry hole under the bridge and it was now safely stowed in his newspaper bag. He was almost on a high as he cycled down the road. These were his last minutes of freedom and, somehow, he had to get through to the barracks before he was caught. Then his mission would be accomplished; he would not have let Duncan down. Later, he would have to think what it would be like to be banged up.

Some of the older boys from the home had been in prison and they had given him some graphic accounts. Of course, he didn't believe half of what they said, but even half was bad enough. The loss of privacy, the awful routine, the endlessness of it, began to strike home to him as he cycled along. Gradually he was left with a sense of terrible foreboding. Almost immediately the feeling was replaced by a dreadful sense of loss, and he now knew that he couldn't bear life without Kathy, despite all the high ideals of the note that he had written to her. The morning was grey and cloudy and there was a chilly little breeze. His life suddenly seemed quite purposeless.

Kathy saw the mouth organ, lying on the floor by the sardine tin, quite a long time later. Gingerly she picked it up and looked at its battered shape. Everything had begun with this ordinary-looking instrument. Then she saw a serrated edge. No, it looked more like teethmarks. Suddenly, Kathy had a horrible feeling. Would they have allowed Jack to go to the gallows with his beloved mouth organ clenched in his teeth? Had he bitten hard on it as the rope cut into his neck? It was a strange thought. But if it had happened, had Jack's power of love and hatred been blown into the mouth organ in one large, long, despairing and expiring breath?

The roads were very empty as Steve cycled up the long straight hill that led to the barracks. A milk cart rattled by and some early workers passed him, heads down and miserable. Of the police, there was no sign. Was the luck still with him? Gradually he neared the barracks and was within spitting distance of it when he sensed rather than saw the police car turn the corner at the bottom of the road. The driver was crawling slowly, intent on checking every drive. Then he heard the sound of another as it nosed its way into the barracks security zone from a side street. With great presence of mind Steve flung himself and his bike into some bushes at the side of the road. He lay there with the wheels spinning, wondering if he had dashed himself far enough off the road. Soon he heard the sound of the police car's engine purring slowly past, and he knew that for a moment he was safe.

For a while he lay there, exhausted. Then Steve began to weigh up the consequences of two opposing lines of action. He could deliver the joke device for his brother now – and be caught immediately – or let him down and do a bunk. Steve lay in the thick bushes, breathing in their musty scent and watching the silvery spiders' webs glisten in the watery sunshine that was trying to break through the clouds. Slowly he came to the obvious conclusion. Prison, he could not bear; his brother's wrath and his sense of betrayal, he could – so he would do a bunk. Beyond the bushes stretched great tracts of heathland with clumps of trees as cover. He would leave his bike but he'd better take Duncan's joke bomb with him – it was too dodgy to leave around. Slowly Steve clambered stiffly to his feet. He felt totally exhausted but the thought of freedom gave him new strength. He would run and hide and go on running and hiding until he could get over the sea. He fancied Spain. Then, after the hue and cry had died down, he might be able to steal back and see Kathy. In his desperation Steve refused to see the fantasy of it all. He wanted freedom above anything, and with all the instincts of a trapped animal he would fight his way towards it.

Gradually Steve inched his way out of the bushes, looking round cautiously to see if the coast was clear. It was – at least to the first group of trees. Steeling himself, Steve burst into a run across the sandy soil, literally throwing himself into the trees. Then, peering cautiously out, he saw that his first run was undetected. He lay in the shelter of the pines for a long time before he screwed up his courage to make the dash to the next copse. And so, for the rest of the morning, Steve made his way over the heathland in dashes and long waits. As he made his jerky way, Steve saw in his mind's eye the prison cell, and that was what spurred him, despite the beginnings of a hunger and a thirst that were soon to rise to monumental proportions.

Kathy crawled out of the sanctuary with the mouth organ and Steve's note in the back pocket of her jeans. It was ten o'clock and she had slept for some hours. Now the time had come to give herself up. She was very conscious that she was filthy and she was equally certain that she smelt awful. The sky was grey and the sun was still struggling to shine through the clouds.

The scene below was startling. There were policemen, policewomen and dogs everywhere. There was a police caravan, loads of trucks and Land-Rovers and cars. The grounds were severely trampled and the wilderness had been thrashed down with machetes. For a few moments Kathy just stood by the sanctuary and looked down, first on the house, which also appeared to be full of policemen, and then on the grounds. Then someone looked up and she waved calmly.

'You can stop looking,' she called. 'I'm over here.'

Kathy sat in the caravan drinking a cup of hot sweet tea, giving an edited version of what she and Joe and Steve had been up to. She left out the mouth organ and the bees and the past fusing with the present, and once she had learnt, to her immense relief, that Joe was going to be all right, she minimised the ferocity of the attack Steve had made on him. Kathy was interviewed by an intense young policewoman who kept asking her if she had been 'interfered with'. And Kathy kept repeating very firmly: 'No, I've not been "interfered with".'

'Now this Tully boy.'

'Who?'

'Steven Tully.'

'Oh, Steve.'

The policewoman frowned slightly and Kathy wondered if she was thinking that she was just a slag – a well-brought-up girl like her shouldn't have been consorting with two delinquents from a community home. Kathy looked into her eyes. Yes, she *was* thinking just that.

'His brother is outside.'

'Yeah?'

'Very worried about him. Apparently he's carrying a bomb.'

Kathy stared at her in bewilderment. This couldn't be

happening. A bomb. Jack? Was the past catching up with them again?

'Did you hear me?'

'Yes.'

'Do you know anything about this?'

'No.'

'Are you certain?' The policewoman's voice was cold.

'Absolutely. What kind of bomb?'

'A small-scale device. Like a letter bomb.'

'Where is it?'

'In his newspaper bag. We've found the bike near the barracks. But no sign of Steven or his bag.'

'You mean he's still carrying it?'

'We think so.'

'But doesn't he realise it could go off?'

'We don't know.'

'What could happen if it went off?'

'At close range? He could be very badly hurt.'

'Killed?'

'I can't say.'

'But *why* was he taking a bomb to the barracks?'

'His brother is still being questioned.'

'Why?' Her voice was desperate.

'I'm afraid I can't say,' the policewoman repeated.

'You mean you *won't* tell me.'

'Listen, Kathy, if you want to help Steven, tell me where he is.'

'I don't know.'

'Where might he run?'

'I tell you I don't know – if I did, I'd tell you. Don't you think I would?' Now her voice was contemptuous.

'Do you realise the seriousness – '

'Yes. And I . . .'

But she was interrupted by the opening of the caravan

door. Mum and Gran stood on the threshold with a policeman. Mum looked terrified and Gran looked in her element. Gloating.

Tim sat down beside Joe's bed. He was looking better.

'Kathy's been found.'

'Is she OK?' His voice was still a rasping whisper but it was clearer.

'Yes. Fine. No damage at all.'

'Great. Steve?'

'On the run.' Tim didn't tell him any more, although he knew everything. 'They'll get him.'

'What will they do to him?'

'We'll have to see. He'll need support.'

'Yeah.' Joe didn't sound enthusiastic. 'Can I see her?'

'Soon.'

'Why not now?'

'She's being questioned.'

Joe closed his eyes. 'We did a house.'

'I know.'

'I didn't lay a finger on her.'

'No,' said Tim.

'Do you believe me, Tim?'

'Of course.'

'You don't, do you?'

'Relax, Joe.' He got up.

'Where you going?'

'To look for Steve.'

'When do I see her?'

'Soon. Now try and rest.'

Tim went out quickly and Joe lay back and closed his eyes. Soon explanations would be needed. Blimey, he thought. I could be explaining things for the rest of my natural.

* * *

'She's always been a difficult girl.' Predictably Gran was the first to condemn as Kathy sat in the police caravan, surrounded by her critics. The policewoman shook her head tersely as if in agreement. Mum looked shattered and Kathy knew that she had been letting Gran get on top of her.

'Are you all right, love?' asked Mum.

'Yes – I ran away with Joe. He looked after me.'

'I bet he did,' snarled Gran.

The policewoman returned to her inquisition, her pale narrow face set in official concentration. I wonder if she's ever felt like running away? thought Kathy.

'Now, Kathy, you must try and think. Where might Steve be?'

She looked at her watch. It was midday. She wondered how far he had got. 'I don't know, do I?' she replied tersely. 'I keep telling you – I *don't know* where he is.'

Steve had made a bivouac. He had covered some miles of heathland that morning, but now he was so exhausted he knew he could go no further.

He had crawled into a little copse which contained bracken and low branches and, uprooting some of the bracken, he had built himself a shelter. He slept throughout the afternoon – a deep and dreamless sleep – and when he woke in the early evening he felt totally refreshed. Gradually, as he lay there, the events of the previous day returned to him and he felt as if he was going to be sick. His hatred of Joe had now completely died and he could hardly understand why he had nearly killed him. When he thought of Kathy he felt a kind of sharp pain and he knew that that pain was his love for her. Then he thought of what would happen if he was caught, and instinctively he got to his feet. He must move on. But to where? Now that he was fresher and clearer in his mind he knew that he had been running blindly and hadn't the faintest idea where he was. Soon he was bound to come to a main road and then he would be exposed again. Also, it was more than possible that he was running and walking in a complete circle. He was lost and the pain he felt for Kathy was beginning to be replaced by an ever sharper and more throbbing pain. The pain of hunger. What the hell was he to do?

'The public is warned not to approach this young man as he is highly dangerous.'

Kathy switched off the radio unbelievingly. Could they really be talking about the Steve she knew? But the Steve she knew had beaten Joe to a near pulp and was carrying some kind of bomb. So yes, he was highly dangerous and, even now, a policeman was standing guard outside her house. She had been allowed home 'pending further questioning', which sounded very ominous and probably was. Quite what kind of trouble she was going to get into, she had no idea, but ever since she had been home, she had been confined to her room and surrounded by the continuous 'told you so-ing' of Gran. But at least she had been allowed a bath and she knew that Joe was going to be all right. She had asked if she could see him, but had been soundly refused by everyone. Even the young policeman had only been marginally sympathetic. 'You mustn't see him, love,' he had tried to explain. 'It's just not on. We don't want you associating at all.' And Gran had added whenever she could, 'If you mix with trash, what do you expect?'

Kathy had not had the energy to argue and now, as

she dozed on her bed, she allowed herself the luxury of a sleeping-waking dream about Joe's village by the sea, and once again she saw herself lying in the dunes with him. As she finally slept, she dreamt of making love to him properly. It was all so perfect and he was so gentle. Then a big seagull flew overhead and settled next to them. It had a cruel sharp beak and a wary eye that she recognised as belonging to Gran. It began to peck at Joe's face and there was nothing they could do to beat the bird off. Then the gull suddenly revealed a tiny pair of wizened hands that it unfurled from somewhere in its feathers. The tiny hands went round Joe's neck with incredible strength and began to strangle him. As she tried to wrest them away, Kathy knew the hands belonged to Gran.

Duncan had spent the day being grilled jointly by both civil and military police, who were horrified by what he had been planning.

'You get your teenage brother to deliver a letter bomb full of plastic explosive to a clerk in the barracks who, in all innocence, was going to place it in your Commanding Officer's locker? It's incredible.' They looked at him aghast and so strangely that he wondered if they thought him mad.

'He doesn't know it's got plastic in it. I told him it was a practical joke, a fire cracker, there'd be a bit of a bang. Enough to scare.' Duncan babbled desperately, but his mind was elsewhere. So far they had not caught on to the connection between him and Steve and Mr Sandey's car, but they would in time and he had to protect himself from further revelations. Then, just as he was being grilled again by another and higher-ranking military policeman, Duncan had a brainwave. He was going to have to face a court martial and probably a prison sentence. Thank God, his parents were dead. They would never have lived through this, with their pride and their generations of army background. But how was he going to live through prison? It would, no doubt, be peopled by hundreds of Catchpoles. If they thought he was mad, then he would be mad. It should be easy enough, and a stay in a psychiatric unit would be a damn sight better than a spell in prison.

'And you wanted to take your revenge on this Catchpole character by stitching him up for the planting of the bomb?' The military policeman's voice was full of incredulity.

'Oh yes,' hastily improvised Duncan. 'You see, Catchpole and those like him do not walk in the way of the Lord. And neither does the CO. I didn't want to kill anyone,' Duncan added hastily, 'but if they will not walk in the way of the Lord they must receive warnings.'

'I see,' said the military policeman, writing furiously in his notebook. 'Now we're getting somewhere.'

Yes, thought Duncan. We certainly are.

Steve walked down the country lane. In fact, he staggered, the hunger pangs gnawing at him and his feet sore and impossibly painful. He felt dizzy and depressed: he had seen a sign pointing to a village only a few miles from Camberley, so he had probably been walking in a circle. Suddenly the dizziness increased and he felt he was going to fall. Looking at his watch, Steve saw that it was seven in the evening. He sat down – almost fell down – and lay in a ditch by the side of the road. He began to sob.

* * *

'Kathy.'

'Mmm?'

She woke to see Mum sitting on the edge of her bed, a cup of tea in one hand and a plateful of jam sandwiches in the other. Mum wore a conspiratorial grin that said it's you and me against the world. And the world was Gran. She put a finger to her lips and winked at Kathy. A dusty sunbeam inched its way through the curtains and caught Mum's head in a blazing halo of light. For a second she looked like a goddess.

'Sshh – she's asleep.'

'Gran?'

'Like an old lizard. Curled up in the sunlight.'

'She's been rotten about this.'

'She's an old woman who can't change.'

'I hate her – '

'So do I sometimes. But she's my mum and I love her. Despite the fact that she's an old scallywag.'

'I wouldn't describe her that way.'

'I would.' There was a pause and the room seemed suddenly very cold as if the sun had gone behind a big cloud. 'Did they touch you? Those two?'

'Neither of them. They think too much of me.'

'And what do you think of *them*?'

'I love Joe.'

'And the other boy? The boy with the bomb?'

'He was like a father to me. He looked after me.'

'He could have killed you.' But there was no venom in Mum's voice as she put the food and drink down on the bedside table. Kathy gazed at her in amazement. This wasn't the old leaden, Gran-dominated Mum she was talking to, nor even the Mum who talked secrets in the Brown Owl. This was a new Mum who was more like a sister.

'I want you to have a good rest and then we'll talk,' she said.

'Talk?' Kathy stared at her in amazement.

'Yes – I want to talk about your two blokes. Through them – ' she hesitated ' – I'll know you as a woman.'

Kathy's eyes filled with tears as her arms reached out for her mother. They clung to each other on the bed.

'I'll learn. I'll learn,' they both whispered at the same time.

When Mum had gone, Kathy lay on her bed, feeling wide awake, bathed in a slowly creeping glow of contentment, sipping her tea and wolfing down the sandwiches. Her thoughts alternated between Joe and Steve. Then she shifted her weight, feeling something biting at her from her back pocket. She pulled it out and found that she was staring down at the battered mouth organ. Instinctively she brought it to her lips.

Dimly Steve caught the low whine of the car engine and huddled further into the ditch as he heard it rattle to a stop a few centimetres away from him. It was the police. It must be. He half rose and then fell back again. Let them take him. He had no strength left.

Joe tossed and turned on the hard hospital bed as he heard the approach of a deep-throated car engine. A car? In a ward? He heard a door slam and feet approaching down the corridor.

Kathy squirmed further into the bed as half-sleep overtook her. She heard the sound of a rattling car engine outside the house. It must be the police again. Then she heard steps on the garden path but no knock at the door.

The footsteps were coming up the stairs. They were very heavy and could not possibly belong to Mum or Gran. Perhaps the front door was open. But why was there no mumble of conversation? And where was Mum? The door opened. Kathy screamed.

Part Six
DEAD RECKONING

The Alvis stood by the roadside, its engine gently ticking over and its chrome and bodywork gleaming in the evening sunlight. The young man stood by the ditch, looking down at Steve. He was dressed in a long leather motoring coat and cap and looked vaguely familiar.

'Who are you?'

'Jack Tully's the name.'

'Yeah?'

'Are you ready?'

'Ready?'

'Come on, old son. We've got to make a delivery.'

Steve stared up at him, totally confused.

'I don't get you.'

The young man gave him a thin smile. 'We have to be at the house in half an hour.' He leant down a leather-gloved outstretched hand.

'Where?'

'At Woodenbridge. The band are already playing. Are you coming?'

Steve knew he had no choice as he was drawn up out of the ditch.

'Who are you?' asked Kathy, sitting up in bed.

'Jack Tully's the name.' The young man was dressed in a long leather motoring coat and cap.

'Who?'

'Are you ready?'

'What are you doing in my bedroom?' Her voice was shrill with fear.

'Come on, old girl. We've got to make a delivery.'

'What delivery?'

He gave her a thin and irritable smile. 'We have to be at the house in half an hour.' He stretched out a leather-gloved hand.

'Where?'

'At Woodenbridge. The band are already playing. Are you coming?'

Kathy knew she had no choice as she was drawn towards him.

'Who the hell are you?'

'Jack Tully's the name.'

Joe stared incredulously at the young man in his strange coat and cap.

'Who?'

'Are you ready?'

'Ready for what?'

'Come on, old son. We've got to make a delivery.'

'Eh?'

The young man gave him a thin and irritable smile. 'We have to be at the house in half an hour.' He threw out a leather-gloved outstretched hand.

'Where we going? I mean – I can't go anywhere. Haven't you noticed this is a hospital?'

'To Woodenbridge. The band are already playing. Are you coming?'

Joe rose stiffly from his bed. He knew he had no choice.

Steve was soon convinced that he was dreaming, as the Alvis purred through the country lanes. He sat beside Jack, while in the rear seats were Joe and Kathy. Or at least, shadowy people who were rather like them. In fact, nothing was distinct at all, neither the inside of the car nor the outside landscape, which had a muzziness to it where there was no detail and only a blur. Colours seemed translucent and strange sounds assailed them. The firing of guns, the lowing of cattle, a man repeating a prayer, the mewing of a gull and all the time Jack, the spectral driver, hummed 'Greensleeves'. All knew themselves to be dreaming for each of the three could sometimes see through Jack to the blurred hedgerows beside him.

Steve staggered towards the bandstand. All was in confusion; nothing was as it seemed.

'Hurry up,' said Jack in Kathy's mind. 'We can't stay around here. Let's go and have some tea.' They were walking in dappled sunlight to a hubbub of distorted noise. Joe was no longer with them. Wasn't he playing in the band?

The light seemed wrong. So did distances. Sometimes Steve could see the bandstand quite near and at other times it seemed a long way away. The newspaper bag round his shoulders felt so heavy – it was dragging him down. His shoes felt as if there were lead weights in them and each step across the blinding white gravel was physically painful. The landscape had a bleached, burnt-out look to it and everything, everything was so white. He turned. Woodenbridge behind him was black, like a negative, and the bandstand in front of him a blazing white which almost blinded him. He staggered on over the dazzling gravel and then found himself on grass that looked like ashes. No music came from the bandstand, no one was there, and it was beginning to feel like early morning.

Joe and Kathy stood hand in hand on the flattened wilderness of grass and scrub that had once been the sweeping lawns of Woodenbridge. It was early evening and a rainbow arced the sky whilst gentle summer rain fell refreshingly on their faces. Why were they here? Why were they watching Steve walk so slowly, so painfully through the grass towards nothing at all. They had no knowledge of how they had come here and Joe looked awfully ill, with his blackened face and the lint bandage at his neck.

'You ought to sit down,' she said. But he shook his head, his eyes fixed determinedly on Steve's back.

'Where the hell is he going?' he rasped. 'What does he think he's doing?'

'He's digging something out of his newspaper bag.'

'Looks like a box,' said Joe in an abstracted whisper.

'How did we get here?' asked Kathy, bemused.

Joe shook his head irritably. Steve was bending down now and thrusting the box under the bandstand.

'That's right,' repeated Jack, who was standing close by. 'Open it in sixty seconds. Well done, old son. You learn well.' He drew up the collar of his motoring coat and shivered.

'You cold?' asked Steve. He felt much better now, as if a great weight had been taken from his body.

'I'm perpetually cold.' Jack shivered again.

'He's talking to someone.'

'Just muttering to himself,' rasped Joe. He put a hand to his neck.

'He was looking at someone.'

'Looking into space.' Joe rubbed his neck again.

'Why are you *here*? Why are *we* here?'

He shrugged. 'Search me.'

'I've got no memory of leaving home,' she whispered. 'I can't remember *coming* here. And you should be in bed. You'll be ill.' She tried to stifle a sob and failed. She tightened her grip on Joe's hand. 'I love you,' she said.

But he didn't reply. Joe was staring ahead with great intensity. He was watching Steve.

Jack had gone. Steve was alone. The bandstand was caught up in swirling mist and the bleached whiteness was even more intense. He climbed up on the bare boards of the bandstand and tried to see further over the valley. But the light was too bright. Whiteness was everywhere. He couldn't see a thing.

'What are we going to *do*?' Kathy had detached her hand from Joe's and was sitting on the grass in a sobbing heap. 'I wasn't meant to leave my room.'

But Joe was still staring ahead.

'What are you looking at?'

'Steve's gone barmy. Look at him. He's walking round and round a patch of grass. I'm going over there.'

'No!'

'Why?' For the first time he looked down at her.

'I don't know. He might attack you. Again.'

'He looks as if he's drunk – or high. Look at his eyes. They're kind of – weird.'

'Stay.'

'Look – '

'Please!'

But Joe moved away, taking a few steps towards Steve.

'No!' she screamed, reached out and grabbed him round the legs. As he fell, heavily, she saw Steve was under the bandstand now, opening the box. A brilliant white flash came from where Steve was crouching. There was a great billow of hot air and she saw him on the ground, writhing, while flames licked at his legs. Kathy felt in her back pocket and instinctively dragged out the mouth organ. She knew what was happening. She had seen it at school. Kathy blew into the mouth organ and saw it all again. The bandstand was blowing up, the bandsmen were falling about, some of their legs had come off. Legs and arms and bits of body. There was smoke and flames and it was all just as she had seen it at school. She moved and felt Joe's leg against hers. Then she turned round, for no reason, and saw Jack. He was running towards the walled garden. She looked up and saw the swarm. The bees. The black cloud was following him. She put down the mouth organ. Joe was still there, but Steve was getting up. There was blood all over his face. It kept pumping out. She heard a buzzing sound and looked up. There was a black cloud directly above Steve's head, high in the air, following his dragging, swaying steps towards the walled garden.

Kathy pulled Joe to his feet. He was sweating profusely and his hands were shaking. Once he was on his feet, she began to propel him along.

'Where are we going?' he asked plaintively, like a small boy being dragged to retribution.

'The walled garden,' she gasped out, 'before the soldiers get there.' Kathy picked up the mouth organ and put it back in her pocket. She would take it back to where it belonged.

She knew he was very badly hurt as she walked down the path in the walled garden towards him. He was black all over and the blood kept pouring from his head. The swarm of bees hovered over the rotting hives in the walled-garden wilderness and she threw the mouth organ across to him. It landed at his feet but he did not look at her as he picked it up. Steve put it to his lips. No sound seemed to come directly from the mouth organ but the garden was pervaded with the sound of 'Greensleeves'. Kathy watched as the swarm of bees descended until they were hovering amongst the last remnants of the wood of the hive. Wild flowers confused the garden now, a riot of jumbled colour, flooding the summer evening with a honeysuckle-dominated aroma. But there were wild roses also and meadowsweet and ragwort and clover. She could smell herbs too, marjoram, basil and thyme. The garden seemed to bounce the sound of the mouth organ around its walls so that echo followed echo until the clematis-hung masonry began to vibrate with the sweet, sad notes.

'What have you done?' Her voice pierced the musical resonance as he knew it would. It had only been a matter of time. 'What have you done?'

Steve continued playing, listening to her padding over the grass towards him. There was hardly a sound except the crunch of her foot on the occasional dead and dry rose briar. The buzzing of the bees seemed to fill his head along with the music, blotting out everything else.

'What have you done?' she kept saying over and over again. Then she demanded, 'Do you *know* what you've done?' He felt her beside him now, her breath coming in tiny gasps. She gave a little whinny of hysterical laughter.

'Why, you're fiddling while Rome burns!' As she laughed, she hit him hard round his blackened, bloodied face, time and time again. He bent away from her blows, too intent on watching the bees to really face the reality of her loathing. The mouth organ flew out of his mouth, jarring his teeth, and fell on the grass. Kathy picked it up.

'Put it back,' Steve whispered. 'Put it back in the hive.'

Hurriedly Kathy ran through the long grass and found the rotting hive, huddled against the mellow brick of the wall. She thrust the mouth organ through the broken wood and stood up, the sweat running down her face. Then she saw that Joe was standing there.

As Steve turned away from them, back towards the bees, the soldiers were running through the archway, pointing their guns at him. As they did so, the swarm of bees rose high above the garden, forming a tight black cloud in the fading evening heat. Then they flew away. As Kathy clung tight to Joe's hand, the landscape of Woodenbridge shimmered and grew indistinct. Then they both smelt ozone and heard the sound of the sea.

'Steve's going to live. Bad burns to the hands and face and lacerations to the head,' Tim told his wife. 'That brother of his only put in enough plastic explosive to maim but Steve's still lucky, considering the range.'

'And Joe?' she asked anxiously.

'They're discharging him tomorrow. Funny thing though – '

'What's that?'

'When Joe and Kathy came out of that walled garden they had strands of wet seaweed round their necks.'

* * *

Kathy and her mum were sitting on the side of a dried-up fountain in the shopping precinct.

'Soon be time to get back for Gran,' said Mum, looking at her watch.

'Let's just have five more minutes.'

'All right.'

'It's so good to be together. To have talked.'

A dog trotted past, saw the fountain, paused and lifted his leg. They both laughed.

'We don't half choose some lousy places to have our five minutes in,' said Mum.

'I don't care where we go,' said Kathy, 'as long as we're together. Sometimes.'

'Won't you want to be with Joe?'

'Not if he gets between us.'

'He won't.' Mum smiled. 'I wouldn't let that happen.'

'What about Gran?'

'She'll have to know her place.'

'She won't like that.'

'I'll have to stand up to her, won't I?'

'Mum – '

'Yes, my darling?'

'Could we ever go on holiday? You and me and Joe?'

'I don't see why not. I'd have to find a Gran-sitter, though.'

'Can you?'

'I can try. Where do you want to go?'

'I want to find somewhere in Ireland. Somewhere that looks like – somewhere I dreamt of.'

'That might be a hard search.'

'Yes – but it's the searching that counts, isn't it?'

Also available by Anthony Masters

BADGER

'If you tell,' Jenny threatened, 'I'll never speak to you again!'

'What is it?' demanded Andrew.

'It's Dad! Dad – and the terriers. He sends them down after the badgers.'

'What!'

'Yes –' Jenny's voice shook as she repeated the sentence.

'He sends them down after the badgers.'

A bit of country air, that's what Andrew's visit to his relatives is supposed to be for. Instead he finds himself mixed up in a bitter family crisis. Instinctively, Andrew joins sides with his cousin, Jenny, against her father's 'hobby' of badger-baiting. But there's more to the conflict than that. Somehow, Uncle George's persecution of the badgers is linked with a jealous hatred of Jenny's mysterious friend, Brock . . .

Starling Point Series

Starling Point is a South London housing estate, bubbling with streetwise life. It is also the title of a series of vivid and exciting stories about the people who live there.

STREETWISE

Sam's father, a policeman, has been killed. Driven to find out the facts behind the death for himself, Sam makes two important discoveries. His father had ruthless enemies – and he was leading a kind of double life.

Caught up in a dangerous chain of events, Sam undergoes a powerful and shocking voyage of discovery . . .

A novel of uncompromising honesty that tackles issues of prejudice and corruption head-on.

Starling Point Series

ALL THE FUN OF THE FAIR

Jim North and his Gallopers – a beautifully painted and carved fairground ride – have an annual date at the Starling Point estate. But this year they have not bargained for the dramatic end of Gerry Kitson's mystery ride, nor the arrival of their new assistant, Leroy. And as Leroy desperately tries to prove himself, the battle to save the Gallopers, not only from bankruptcy but also from vandalism, begins.

Starling Point Series

CAT BURGLARS

CAT, is a huge Persian cat. He's Mrs Willard's pride and joy, the favourite of the twenty that live in her flat at Starling Point. He's also a ferocious menace.

When Mick Newby befriends Mrs Willard he does not know she has a secret behind the locked door in her flat. He soon discovers what it is. And when he confides in Leroy and Gallica, Mrs Willard's secret begins to invade their lives . . .